## About the Author

Thomas Rowan is a father of three and lives in Wisconsin serving in the Air National Guard. Apart from reading and writing, Thomas spends most of his free time on various hobbies including painting, fitness, and martial arts.

Love is Blind

# Thomas Rowan

## Love is Blind

Olympia Publishers
*London*

www.olympiapublishers.com
OLYMPIA PAPERBACK EDITION

Copyright © Thomas Rowan 2023

The right of Thomas Rowan to be identified as author of
this work has been asserted in accordance with sections 77 and 78 of
the Copyright, Designs and Patents Act 1988.

All Rights Reserved

No reproduction, copy or transmission of this publication
may be made without written permission.
No paragraph of this publication may be reproduced,
copied or transmitted save with the written permission of the publisher,
or in accordance with the provisions
of the Copyright Act 1956 (as amended).

Any person who commits any unauthorised act in relation to
this publication may be liable to criminal
prosecution and civil claims for damage.

A CIP catalogue record for this title is
available from the British Library.

ISBN: 978-1-80074-717-3

This is a work of fiction.
Names, characters, places and incidents originate from the writer's
imagination. Any resemblance to actual persons, living or dead, is
purely coincidental.

First Published in 2023

Olympia Publishers
Tallis House
2 Tallis Street
London
EC4Y 0AB

Printed in Great Britain

# Acknowledgements

Special thanks to Chrisanna Manders. For it was your input and support that made this book, not only possible, but also, the full story it was meant to be. Thank you.

# Chapter 1

## New Girl

"Oof." Kirsten let out a soft grunt as she re-racked the barbell in the bench press.

Kirsten sat up and looked around the gym, bobbing her head slightly to the sound of her music playing through her headphones. The gym was only partially full as it usually was this time in the afternoon on a Saturday. It's not that Kirsten didn't wish she could be doing something else on a beautiful weekend like this one. However, since she had just recently moved to the area, Kirsten didn't know anyone yet, other than a few co-workers. And they weren't the type to do things that Kirsten was interested in on weekends.

While only five feet four inches tall, Kirsten was very athletic with dark brown hair that fell just past her shoulders and blue eyes. At twenty-eight years old, Kirsten was single and enjoyed the time to pursue the activities she desired.

Apart from the gym, some of Kirsten's favorite activities were playing various sports and just hanging with friends, that said, being new to the area, she didn't really have any friends to hang with just yet. South Florida was an entirely new area for Kirsten. Having spent most of her time in the upper east coast, the warm sun and beautiful beaches were a pleasant change of scenery. She had traveled a bit throughout her life, but never this far south, so she was excited to see how her life would take off in this area.

Kirsten's thoughts snapped back as she laid back down to do her next set. When Kirsten sat back up, her thoughts drifted again and went to her current situation. New city, new job, new gym…

"Hey."

Kirsten snapped out of her thoughts and pulled one of her headphones out as she looked up to see who was talking. Kirsten was used to people talking to her in the gym, or at least attempting to talk to her. Kirsten would usually acknowledge them just enough to show her annoyance and disinterest and then go about her business. It's not that she didn't like socializing, however, in the gym, being approached by strangers was the last place Kirsten was looking for a conversation.

As Kirsten made eye contact with the individual that had called out to her, she realized it was another young woman around Kirsten's age. She was a little taller than Kirsten but had a similar toned and athletic build. She had brown eyes, and her hair was tied up into a ponytail and was light brown with what looked like blonde highlights throughout. She looked as though she had already had a great workout by the sweat sheen that was on her skin.

Kirsten was shocked at first glance and already had a distaste for her based on the initial appearance. *Just someone looking for more attention than an actual workout,* Kirsten thought when she saw this woman standing there. Partly because she didn't recall seeing her in the gym working out until now, and partly because of her appearance in the scantily clad gym outfit and perfectly done hair. The outfit consisted of what was barely considered full coverage booty shorts and a sports bra that looked like it just barely fit. Overall, it was probably just borderline with the rules on what kind of gym attire was allowed to be worn in here.

Comparatively, Kirsten was more modestly dressed, with just some capri leggings and full coverage sports bra top.

"Hey," the woman repeated now that Kirsten was looking at her.

Kirsten didn't hide her disinterest as she responded. "Hey." She was sure all this woman was going to ask her was when she was finished so she could use the equipment that Kirsten was currently on. Or, worse yet, talk to her and end up ruining the rest of the workout Kirsten had set up for herself.

"Hey, I saw you struggling to make that last set," the woman said. "Do you want me to help spot you?"

"Oh. Sure. Thank you," Kirsten said as her tone changed, and she responded more naturally.

"You're welcome. My name is Allison, by the way."

Kirsten tucked her earpiece that she had removed into her shirt leaving the one in her right ear still in. She laid down to get ready for her next set before responding. "I'm Kirsten," she finally said as she got in position.

Once she was finished, the girls talked a bit more and realized they had some similar interests. Both had similar music tastes, enjoyed the same kind of workouts, and liked the same movies and other casual activities. Allison joined Kirsten to finish out her workout, and Kirsten was pleasantly surprised that her initial perception of Allison was somewhat wrong. Allison indeed was more of a flirt and liked the attention; however, at the same time, she still actually put in the work to push herself in the gym.

"I'm curious," Kirsten said as she switched out on the cable machine to let Allison get a turn.

"About what?" Allison asked.

"What were you doing when you walked up to me at the

bench?" Kirsten said. "I don't remember seeing you before that anywhere."

"I was running," Allison stated as she finished her set. "I decided to go running on the treadmill before my lifting today."

"Oh, yep. That would be why I didn't see you," Kirsten said, laughing as she did.

The cardio room was its own separate room within the gym off to the side. It had two doors with small windows of entrance and exit into the main part of the gym. However, the only window in that room came from the exterior wall facing the parking lot. So, unless you walked into the cardio area, or someone came or went while you were in the main part of the gym, no one would know who was there if they just stayed on the weights side.

As the girls prepared to leave, Allison was already planning a follow-up get together. "Do you live here? Or are you just visiting?" Allison asked as they reached her car.

"I just moved here last week," Kirsten responded.

"Oh, very nice! I was going to say that I don't recall seeing you around here before," Allison said.

"Yea, I've only just been getting into my routine here. Trying to get used to my schedule with work and my other hobbies," Kirsten said.

Allison was already in her car and rolling the window down to continue talking to Kirsten. "Nice. Well, do you wanna hang out again sometime?"

"Sure," Kirsten answered. The girls exchanged contact information and parted ways.

Over the next few weeks, the girls hung out regularly. A dinner or a night out drinking on the weekends and talking throughout the week. Kirsten was relieved to have found Allison, although Allison was more of a party girl than Kirsten was. That said, Allison proved to be a good wingman whenever they went out.

Kirsten enjoyed hanging out with Allison since it allowed her to get familiar with the area and network a bit meeting some new people. Some of the evenings would get out of Kirsten's comfort zone. However, no matter how drunk either of them were, no matter what kind of mess they got into, Allison always made sure that they both made it home safe, which was good for Kirsten, who occasionally needed that since she wasn't much of a partier.

Kirsten found out that she can't hold her liquor much, and on one occasion in particular, almost disregarded all safe practices as she was too drunk to even care about what she was doing or with whom. Thankfully, Allison, though still drunk herself, managed to "rescue" Kirsten from that possibly unfortunate circumstance before anything terrible happened. Since then, Kirsten of course took it much slower whenever they went out, making sure that even if they got drunk to have fun, she never lost her wits again.

"You need to come," Allison pleaded as the girls were enjoying a beautiful day on the beach. Kirsten was next to Allison, trying to enjoy the sun, lying out on her towel. It was a beautiful day in the late summer, and possibly one of the last good beach days for a while. So the girls decided to spend the day there and browse the local beachfront shops and such. College classes were just starting and so of course part of the reason they were there was to see the new faces that where in the area for school now. "Boy-toy trolling," is what Allison called it. A silly game of finding eye-candy in the younger college-age guys that usually floated around the beach areas.

And against the wishes of Kirsten, Allison had decided to

keep persisting with her attempts to get Kirsten to join her for a fundraiser that Allison had also mentioned would be when Kirsten would be set up with one of Allison's friends Gabriel. Kirsten had heard Gabriel's name mentioned by Allison before in a few of their conversations.

It seemed that the shipping company that Allison worked for, worked in conjunction with a firm that Gabriel oversaw. Owner or manager, Kirsten wasn't sure, she blanked on some of the details from the past conversations they had. All Kirsten knew for sure was that he was a few years older than her; and Allison knew him through work-related affairs.

"I don't know," said Kirsten, still lying on her back, trying to ignore the question. "It's not my scene, and I'm not looking for a relationship right now. Why don't you just date him?"

"I thought about that back when I first met him. But as I got to know him through work, I realized it wouldn't work," Allison said. "And I know you're not looking, but you never know. And from what I know of him, you two might be good together." Allison continued, "Besides, if after you meet and you don't think it'll work, you're not obligated to date him." Allison chuckled as she finished.

Kirsten was still hesitant, however, Allison seemed to always find a way to make Kirsten fold. Kirsten sat up and faced Allison now. "I suppose," she said, some reluctance still in her voice. Allison about jumped for joy as Kirsten put a finger up in warning.

"I will give him this chance, but I make no promises," Kirsten said, trying to make herself sound serious.

Internally, Kirsten was somewhat excited; she hadn't dated anyone for some time now. And she figured since she'd been here now for a couple months, she could enjoy a date night or two if the right person came along. Part of Kirsten's hesitancy was that she was in a new area and didn't really know the people here. But going through Allison as a way to meet a mutual friend seemed the best route considering her natural resistance to the idea.

Allison practically shouted, "Perfect! You won't hurt my feelings any if it doesn't work."

Kirsten nodded in agreement. "So, when is this big party?"

"Next Saturday," Allison answered. "And it's not just a party; it's a fundraiser. There's going to be a lot of companies represented here. Lots of money, and lots of fancy men and women."

"Okay, fundraiser," Kirsten corrected herself, secretly dreading the idea of fancy men and women bustling about around her. She never minded getting dressed up for special occasions. However, being familiar with the type of people that would be at this function, Kirsten felt uncomfortable partly due to the fact that she never socialized with this class of people on any basis, let alone would have ever considered, nor been invited to an event of this nature. "What's it for?"

"Some collective charity thing," Allison said. "The company I work for is part of it, but I'm honestly not sure exactly what the money is for. I think it just goes into a collective fund for local charity events."

Kirsten groaned as she rolled her eyes and laid back down on her towel. "Interesting," she said as she exhaled heavily.

"Oh, stop it," Allison said playfully as she laid back down on her towel next to Kirsten's. "It'll be a good time." Kirsten didn't say anything, as she put her sunglasses back up and got comfortable. After a moment, Allison shot back up. "Oh, we should go dress shopping this week after work."

Kirsten gave a smug look glancing up in Allison's direction,

"Really?"

"Yes," Allison said confidently. "We need to look our best and…"

"But I have dresses," Kirsten interrupted.

Allison smiled and laid back down again. "I know, but I want you looking your best for Gabriel."

Kirsten's eyes rolled so hard she thought she could hear them. She turned her head away from Allison and very sarcastically and softly let out a, "Hooray for that."

The next few days flew by leading up to the event. Kirsten wasn't nervous but didn't feel natural either as she and Allison were picking out dresses for the upcoming evening. Being more flirtatious and open, Allison was finding all kinds of more revealing fashions. Kirsten, though finding those options cute and sexy, still preferred to find a more traditional gown, especially given the nature of this function.

The dress Allison chose was a beige color, strapless and full length, but the left side slit came up to the top of the thigh right at the hip, leaving her underwear options either extremely limited, or non-existent. The back material was a sheer fabric that was considered full back coverage in name only; since you could see right through the gown from her tail bone to the upper back. There was a thin line of solid material that ran down the spine, this was to allow for the zipper to be there and have some structure.

At the bottom of her shoulders, it wrapped around under her arms in a strip of solid silken material to cover the chest. The front was the same material except for the strip that wrapped around her breasts from the back. The bottom of the dress was a lightweight solid material with some lace over the top sewn in decorative swirls. After Allison did a few twirls and walked a bit as a test run in the store, she decided it was perfect.

After some time, Kirsten finally found a reasonable outfit that revealed some but left more to the imagination. Her dress was an off-white, slim-fitted gown that reached her mid-calf in length. The slit on the left side went up to her thigh just above the knee. The back was solid, with some decorative lacing down the middle connecting the two sides — spaghetti straps over the shoulders. The front of the dress was laced in a similar netting that Allison's had. However, instead of full open sheer, it made a teardrop shape over her stomach, which tapered nicely under her breasts and met together in between them.

Once the girls found the dresses, they did some shopping for accessories. Afterwards, the girls got some dinner and went about the rest of their evening. Saturday was a few days away yet, and Kirsten was getting more reluctant about going. She had always felt most comfortable in her jeans or leggings and chilling at home. Not that she didn't enjoy the times that Allison and she had gone out, and she liked to socialize and such. But the extravagance about this event made Kirsten slightly uneasy.

"Ugh," Kirsten moaned slightly as she tried to adjust her dress and get comfortable.

"What?" Allison asked sarcastically as she was brushing her hair. "You look great."

"It's not the dress," Kirsten replied. "I'm nervous about tonight."

"The event? Or meeting Gabriel?"

"Both."

"Try not to think about it too much," Allison said as she switched from doing her hair to applying makeup. "You'll be fine, and I'll be right there to help get you through it."

# Chapter 2

# Gabriel

The girls had spent most of the day at Kirsten's place getting ready for the evening. This process usually involved lots of laughter as the two would share stories and drink some wine to "strengthen the nerves" as Allison would say. Start to finish it usually took a couple hours, though, that was for a typical night out. This time, however, if you included the hair and manicure appointments in the morning — plus, what they did on their own at home — it had turned into an all-day affair for the girls.

Kirsten was the first to finish since she was more conservative with her appearance. Allison, however, took some extra time. Kirsten wasn't sure if Allison took longer because she legitimately needed the extra time to get herself together, or, if it was because she just had poor time management. Once they were finally ready, the girls left in Allison's car. Allison had a nice newer BMW Z4, which she treated like her baby. To Kirsten, this was a car that was well above anything she would ever be able to afford or own. Although, as the girls pulled up to the event, Kirsten noticed that comparatively, Allison's car was on the cheaper end of the ones here.

The girls got their chance to pull up and got out of the car. Allison handed her keys to the valet. Camera flashes were all around the outside of the building. People were taking pictures of the guests and the décor around the site. Kirsten glanced around. *Not quite to the scale of a red-carpet event*, she thought. However, it was still much nicer than she initially anticipated. After Allison was finished with the valet, she came up beside Kirsten, who, by this time was already feeling somewhat awkward and shifted over closer to Allison. As means of assurance, Allison put her right arm through Kirsten's left and casually led them to the steps of the building.

As the girls walked up the stairs, Allison gave Kirsten back her arm as she presented their invitations to the usher at the door. As the girls walked in, the entryway was well lit with decorative lights and various company vendor booths along each side. Going in further, the girls found what would be the main dining room. The other guests were scattered around the place, talking in various small groups. For the most part, each attendee was very well dressed. The men in their various three-piece suits, or fancy dinner dress variations. The ladies were all in fancy gowns of various colors and styles. Most of which, did not look very comfortable to Kirsten.

Of the attendees, Kirsten noticed a wide range of age groups. It was also interesting to note that, at least to Kirsten, they dressed similarly based on their ages. The older gentlemen, appeared to have the more traditional set-up, while the younger men tended to wear a more relaxed version of the typical attire. The same went for the ladies; the older ones had more conservative dresses. While the younger generations, showed a more exquisite style with dresses similar to Allison's and her own.

When girls approached the other end of the dining room, they went out the French doors on the backside, which took them to a balcony that overlooked the garden with stairs on both sides. More guests were roaming around or seated on the various benches. String lights were decoratively hung, and a live band off to one side was playing some soft, instrumental music.

"So, where is this Gabriel?" Kirsten asked as the girls walked further into the garden.

"I haven't seen him yet," Allison responded as she glanced around. "He said he would be here, so I'm sure he will."

"All right." Kirsten exhaled heavily as she answered. "Do you know anyone else here?"

"Not really," Allison said. "I recognize a few people that I've interacted with from other companies, but I don't know them beyond that."

"Gotcha."

The girls wandered through the garden a bit and headed back towards the main building to get their dinner seats. As they walked up the stairs, Allison suddenly stopped in her tracks, putting her arm out to stop Kirsten as well. Kirsten caught herself and shot Allison a look of confusion. Allison met Kirsten's eyes, then nodded gently forward and mouthed, *"There he is."* Kirsten's face flushed instantly as she followed Allison's gaze up the stairs. At the top stood a very handsome man in what looked like a very expensive suit. The girls then continued up the stairs. The man at the top looked directly at the pair and smiled casually as he waited for them to reach him.

"Kirsten, meet Gabriel," Allison said, gesturing her left hand as they reached the steps just below where Gabriel stood.

"Hello," Kirsten said as casually as possible. She had to admit that Gabriel was incredibly attractive. Kirsten was surprised by how much she was drawn to him already. She needed a moment to think briefly to remember how to speak before finally asking, "How are you doing this evening?"

"Doing much better now that we've met," Gabriel said smoothly as he grabbed Kirsten's right hand in his and kissed it softly. "Allison had a lot of good things to say about you."

Kirsten flushed again. "Well, I certainly hope she hasn't given away all my conversation topics."

"Even if she did, I'd be happy to hear your stories again," Gabriel replied. He never took his eyes off her. Kirsten glanced down to compose herself before looking back at Gabriel's face.

Kirsten took another step up to be on the balcony with Gabriel. As she got closer, a wave of his cologne hit her like a brick wall, not in an overpowering way, but with a delightful, full and rich smell that made her want to inhale it more and more. Kirsten's face must have given her away because, without any prompt, Gabriel asked if she liked it.

"I do," Kirsten replied. "Is it cinna…?"

"Cinnamon and cedarwood, yes." Gabriel finished her sentence and smiled.

"I love it."

"Thank you."

Allison just stood back smiling and watching as the couple walked in front of her as they entered the main dining area. Gabriel was a handsome man of average height who was fairly muscular in his ability and his appearance. He had thick, jet-black hair, but you wouldn't always know it since he kept it very well-groomed. His hair went well with his naturally darker skin tone and his dark eyes.

As the trio sat down at the table, Kirsten couldn't keep her eyes off Gabriel. She was surprised by how fast she was smitten and taken aback by just the introduction. Kirsten had had dates in the past and was used to being targeted for compliments and date requests by the men she encountered. However, she never once recalled completely losing all sense of her wits with all her past interactions. Something about Gabriel's presence made

Kirsten weak, and that smell, the scent, was cemented in Kirsten's brain.

The group continued to chat through dinner, making small talk and exchanging stories. Kirsten relaxed more as the conversation went on and felt more comfortable in Gabriel's presence. "Did the shipments arrive on time and in good order?" Allison asked Gabriel after a brief pause from their other conversation topic.

Gabriel was taken slightly off guard by this question as was seen in the expression in his face. "Yes, they did," he said, straightening up in his seat. "But let's not talk work."

"Sorry," Allison said quietly. "I just wanted to know if the changes I had to make to the manifest last minute got processed in time."

Gabriel glanced at Kirsten, then, somewhat annoyed, glanced back at Allison. "Yes. The changes were annotated correctly and on time," he said; his tone was quiet but firm. Kirsten could tell something about that topic Gabriel did not like having to talk about right now. After Gabriel spoke, Allison turned the conversation back to casual topics and the three of them enjoyed the dinner uneventfully.

Kirsten initially brushed off the seemingly random conversation shift from earlier as it seemed that now the two were fine. She didn't see the need to press the matter since she was new to the group. Additionally, Kirsten had truly little knowledge of the exact nature of Allison's job, much less Gabriel's. So, it seemed best that she let it go.

Afterward the dinner, they listened to the various speeches and funding announcements from the companies that donated. Not much of it made sense to Kirsten, not that she minded; she was still stuck on Gabriel. After the speeches, the music and mingling continued until around midnight. Gabriel had just finished introducing her to a few of his colleagues when the people started to disperse casually. "Mr Thompson," Gabriel said loudly as the trio approached. Mr Thompson was a middle-aged man. He was average build and height with a full head of hair, it was short and had some greys around his ears. He turned from the people he was talking with to see who had called him.

"Gabriel," Mr Thompson said smoothly as a big grin appeared on his face. His arms opened as Gabriel's did to greet each other with a hug. "It's been a while," Mr Thompson said as they broke the hug. Gabriel agreed and then turned to introduce the girls.

"Alex, I'd like you to meet Kirsten, and Allison," Gabriel said as he stepped aside to allow them to meet. "Kirsten, Allison, this is Alex Thompson, my business associate."

"Nice to meet you," Alex said as he shook both their hands. "Allison, it nice to finally meet in person. I've seen your name come across my desk a lot lately. Moving up in the world, are we?" he asked playfully. Allison chuckled in response and nodded.

Turning to Kirsten, Alex then asked her what brought her into Gabriel's company. "I'm just Gabriel's date this evening. I've known Allison a while now and she set us up." Kirsten couldn't help but chuckle a bit as she finished. She really didn't know what else to say, she had no clue how to talk to these people and her nerve got the better of her in the moment.

*"Just?"* Alex quipped. "Nonsense," he chuckled. "Allison has done you well, there's no finer man than Gabriel here." Kirsten blushed a little in response. Allison just smiled softly at her, and Gabriel grabbed her hand and chuckled a bit as well. "I hope it all works out well for you," Alex finished.

"So what brings you back into town?" Gabriel asked. "It has to be almost a year since I've seen you."

"My office is being relocated here," Alex responded. "My merger with the WesternTech Inc is just getting started, so I'll be back and forth a bit until that goes through. But I'll be here for the most part. I think you'll like what WesternTech will do for with our west coast dealings once this merger is complete."

Gabriel nodded in agreement but didn't seem to really acknowledge the comment and instead shifted his attention to Kirsten and said, "Alex here owns and operates Thompson Pharmaceuticals."

"It's a small firm," Alex cut in. "But we are growing and branching out more. Thanks to our agreement with Gabriel's company to help with distribution." The group continued to talk for several minutes. Afterward, Gabriel and girls shuffled through to several others and made similar introductions at each stop. There were so many names and faces, Kirsten couldn't remember them all as Gabriel rattled through them. After that very quick but exhausting blur, Kirsten was happy when the three of them spent the last few minutes of the night separate from the rest as the crowd thinned out.

"Should I plan on going home by myself tonight?" Allison asked playfully as the group moved outside the front door. The cameras were gone, and the streets were quieter than it was when they had arrived earlier that evening.

"Uhhh," Kirsten stammered briefly before catching herself.

"You should go home with Allison tonight," Gabriel interjected. "We can hang out again next weekend."

"Oh, okay," Allison said. Then turning to Kirsten, she started to ask, "Are you rea…"

"No," Kirsten said, cutting Allison off and speaking much

harsher than intended. "I want to spend more time with Gabriel tonight."

Allison smiled coyly. "Okay. Don't forget I know where you live," she said, turning to Gabriel waving her finger in his face.

Gabriel put his hands up in playful defense. "No harm will come to her."

"Well, enjoy the rest of your night," Allison said, turning to Kirsten. "Text me if you need anything."

"I will," said Kirsten.

With that, Allison went to the valet, and when her car was dropped off, she got in and headed home. Kirsten and Gabriel talked for a bit longer just outside before finally approaching the valet. The valet brought up a newer, fancy sports car. Kirsten wasn't familiar with the model at first, but it was a beautiful car. As Gabriel opened her door Kirsten had to ask what kind it was. "Maserati GranTurismo MC," Gabriel said as he got in the car. With a quick rev of the engine, the two were off, and they headed out to his place.

Gabriel's place was on the upper floor of a beach condominium. His was a modest flat, however, it was still an upper-level condo on the beach. When they arrived, Gabriel punched in the gate code to access the parking area under the building. Once in the elevator, Gabriel selected his floor and punched in his access code to activate the elevator.

As the pair started to ascend, Gabriel leaned in closer to Kirsten. She already had his hand in hers, but as Gabriel moved in, Kirsten rested her head on his shoulder. Feeling Gabriel's gaze, Kirsten glanced up to look into his eyes. His dark eyes drew her in as she turned her body to face him directly. Gabriel's free hand gently touched her cheek; Kirsten closed her eyes and relaxed her head into his hand.

After a moment, Kirsten let go of Gabriel's other hand and brought it up and grabbed the back of his neck. In a smooth motion without thinking, Kirsten brought her face up to meet his. Gabriel, right on cue, leaned forward and met her with a soft yet firm kiss. One soft kiss became two. Two kisses became a locked make-out session as Kirsten suddenly felt herself get pressed against the wall. Before the couple even got to Gabriel's floor, they were already half undressed. Passion and hands were everywhere as Kirsten and Gabriel connected.

*DING!* came the soft tone from the elevator. The ride stopped, and the doors opened. Quickly and smoothly, Gabriel picked Kirsten up, and as she wrapped her legs around his waist, she still kept her hands on his face and their lips locked together. Gabriel walked to his room, and the two continued their night there.

Kirsten woke up to use the bathroom sometime in the early morning hours. As she came back to bed, she felt a slight headache coming on. Kirsten shrugged it off and saw that Gabriel was still sleeping with his back to her. She reached in her purse and grabbed her phone. After scrolling for a minute, she texted a number that wasn't saved.

*'The weather is looking good.'* — *Kirsten*

Kirsten laid back down and set her phone on silent on the nightstand next to her. Before Kirsten had fallen back asleep, however, the light blinked on her phone to indicate a notification came through. Kirsten opened her phone to find a reply from the number she had just texted.

*'The weather is looking great.'* — *Unknown*

And with that, Kirsten rolled over to hug Gabriel and drifted off.

# Chapter 3

# Questions

*Almost a year later.*

The sun shone warm and bright as it often did this time of year. Kirsten was lying out on the yacht in her swimsuit as she had been during the last couple of days; the white swimsuit she wore left little to the imagination and wasn't something she would normally wear to a public beach. But considering it was just her and Gabriel out here on his boat, she decided to wear something more intimate for him. Early summer in Florida was the perfect season, in Kirsten's opinion; she had lightened her hair a bit with some blonde highlights for the summer, which worked well on her.

Over the last year of the relationship, Kirsten and Gabriel had kept it casual, but steady. They would occasionally spend the night at one or the other's place, and they saw each other a few times a week. This wasn't a problem for Kirsten at first, since when they met, she wasn't even looking for anyone, and it seemed to work for Gabriel, too. They genuinely enjoyed each other's company, but now, Kirsten was feeling like it should move to the next level. It had been a few months since they both expressed their feelings for each other and since then, Kirsten felt like everything was falling into place with him.

"Hey, babe!" Gabriel called as he walked up on deck to greet her. "How's the sun?"

"Sun's great today," Kirsten replied. "This has been a great vacation so far. It has been so nice to get away for a few days and not think much about anything." She chuckled as she finished.

Gabriel stated as he sat down next to her. "I have some bad news." His voice was calm and neutral so Kirsten wasn't overly concerned about this statement. "I have to go on a business trip tomorrow." He pulled Kirsten's sunglasses off her face as she turned her head out of the sun to look at him.

Kirsten sighed; she knew Gabriel's job made him travel occasionally, and thankfully so far, he only had to a couple times briefly. "How long do you think this trip will be?" she asked.

"Shouldn't be more than a few days," Gabriel said. "It's just a conference. The person assigned to go had to drop out last minute, so they called me to fill in."

"Where are you going?"

"Vegas," Gabriel responded as he got up to head back below.

"What about the surprise you told me about?" Kirsten asked sitting up.

Gabriel stopped and turned back to Kirsten, "When I get back," he started to say as he smiled. "I promise."

Kirsten thought about asking to go, but then she remembered that she would have to be back at work the day after tomorrow anyway. Kirsten worked at a small insurance company as the office manager. It was a quiet job and relatively dull to her, but it paid the bills and allowed her a regular schedule and time to invest in her other interests.

Once in the harbor, Gabriel and Kirsten said their goodbyes and parted ways. Before Kirsten was even home, Allison was calling—

"Hey, girl," Allison's voice came through the car speakers.

"What's up, Allie?" Kirsten replied.

"How is your short vaca going?"

"Cut shorter."

"What? What happened? Did you guys get into a fight? Did you break up?" Allison's questions came so fast and blurred that Kirsten had a hard time processing them.

"Hey, hey, slow down, Allie," Kirsten finally cut in, almost laughing. "Everything is fine." Allison had a habit of getting overly excited with any new information whether it be good or bad. If Kirsten was to pick a trait that she couldn't stand about Allison, it would be that one.

After Allison calmed down a bit, Kirsten explained further. "No, everything is fine," Kirsten repeated. "He just got called to fill in on a business trip to Vegas and needed to leave tomorrow. So, we came back a day early so he could make his flight."

"Uh-huh," Allison said suspiciously.

"It's true!" Kirsten responded defensively.

"Okay, okay," Allison replied.

The girls talked for a bit as Kirsten drove to her apartment. They were catching up on things since Kirsten's vacation departure a few days ago. Evening time and rush hour meant it would be some time before Kirsten got home. So, it was nice to kill the time with conversation.

As Kirsten pulled into her apartment complex, she and Allison were finishing up the conversation.

"Are you still available this weekend?" Allison asked before saying goodbye.

"Of course!" Kirsten answered. "I always have time for one of your adventures."

"Awesome!" Allison stated cheerfully. "Talk to you later!" Allison finished as she hung up the phone.

Kirsten went up to her apartment and took a long shower. As

much as she had enjoyed her few days out with Gabriel, it was good to be back in her own home and relax somewhat before getting back in the groove of her usual routine.

Kirsten's apartment was in a gated complex and she had a small one-bedroom. The apartment was very spacious considering its overall small size. As you walked in you found yourself in the living room, directly behind that was the kitchen and to the left down the hall, was the bathroom, and at the end was Kirsten's bedroom. The furniture was comfortable but simple and the décor was minimal since Kirsten didn't like a lot of extra "things" around.

The next day went by as usual; Kirsten got up, ran some errands around town, and attended her Mixed Martial Arts class. She had sent Gabriel a few texts throughout the day. Kirsten didn't expect to get instant replies due to Gabriel traveling. However, he hadn't sent anything to her since his departure that morning. This wasn't necessarily a red flag; but Kirsten was a bit concerned, because she hadn't heard from him since before he left. She tried not to let it bother her, and that night Kirsten settled in early to make sure she'd be ready to go back to work the following day.

*RING! RING! RING!*

Kirsten shot up in her bed! It took her a moment to realize it wasn't her alarm but an incoming call on her phone. As she picked it up, she saw it was just after two a.m.

*RING! RING! RING!*

Kirsten's ringtone kept going as she realized it was Gabriel calling. She quickly swiped the screen to answer.

"Hello," Kirsten said sleepily, still coming to her senses.

"Babe!" came Gabriel's frantic voice on the other end. "Babe!" he repeated. His voice was intense but almost sounded scared. Kirsten had never heard Gabriel sound like this, which put her on edge right away.

"Gabe?" Kirsten responded, now more awake and worried herself. "What's going on?"

"Listen, I don't have a lot of time," Gabriel quickly stated. "Someone at the conference was found dead, and I'm being brought in for questioning. I will hopefully have it cleared up soon. But I may be delayed a day or two," he finished.

"Um, okay," Kirsten answered, now confused even more. "Do you need me to do anything?"

"No. I'll be fine, thank you. I love you."

"Okay. Call me if you need anything. I love you too." Kirsten's voice softened. Hypothetical scenarios in her head went off as the sudden click sound on the phone indicated Gabriel had hung up on his end. Kirsten just sat in her bed, silent for several moments. When the shock had finally left her, she opened her phone and searched for news articles that may lead to some clue about what happened in Vegas.

Kirsten searched and searched. She found a few possibilities. However, any article or news blog Kirsten looked at either didn't have enough information or was too old to be the recent event. She then checked her phone to see what time it was in Vegas — twelve-thirty a.m., interesting. *"Perhaps it's so fresh the media hasn't released it yet,"* Kirsten thought to herself. Or, maybe, it never happened, and he's lying to me. Kirsten quickly dismissed this thought until she had more evidence. Besides, it's Vegas. There are probably dozens of murders and crimes going on. And with that, she attempted to go back to sleep.

Sleep wouldn't come easy, however, as Kirsten tossed and turned in her bed, trying to shut off the thoughts about what just happened. She started to recall some of the memories with

Gabriel from the past year...

... "I love the view," Kirsten said as she looked off the balcony of their resort room.

"It is pretty great, isn't it?" Gabriel responded as he walked up behind Kirsten and gave her a soft hug, resting his head on her shoulder.

"Is this where you take all the girls?" Kirsten asked playfully.

Gabriel just rolled his eyes and sighed as he was about to let go of her.

"I'm just kidding," Kirsten said playfully as she grabbed his arms to hold him there.

Kirsten closed her eyes and leaned her head against his while reaching up with her hand and softly stroked his hair. After a moment, Gabriel relaxed his grip and stepped up to stand beside Kirsten, still keeping one arm wrapped around her lower back. Kirsten then wrapped both arms around his waist and rested her head on Gabriel's chest. All was quiet; Kirsten lost herself in the breeze off the ocean, the smell of Gabriel's cologne, and the sound of his heartbeat.

Gabriel pulled away from Kirsten slightly and glanced down at her. Kirsten met his gaze, and their eyes met. Gabriel's dark eyes looked like tiny black holes, deep and enchanting, pulling everything around them to their central point. Kirsten was caught up in the moment and reached up slightly to kiss Gabriel. Gabriel took the hint and reached down to meet Kirsten as they locked in a passionate kiss.

As they kissed, Gabriel picked Kirsten up, and she wrapped her legs around his waist as she grabbed his face and held her lips against his. Gabriel walked back into the room, carrying Kirsten as he did. They fell on the bed together, lost in the passion of each other…

… Images and sensations about that memory flashed in Kirsten's mind. Everything she saw and felt with Gabriel. The memory stopped as Kirsten's thoughts drifted back to the present. She didn't remember if she slept or not, but Kirsten was already awake when her alarm went off. She laid there for a few moments before shutting it off.

Now very tired, Kirsten forced herself up and out of bed and headed towards the shower. Her head was throbbing again, but the steam was helping her calm down. The hot water felt great as Kirsten stood there, trying to wake up and relax a bit at the same time. Kirsten took a little longer to get ready than usual but still made it to work on time.

As she sat down at her desk, Kirsten checked to see if any notifications had come through: nothing. The office seemed more boring than usual as she stared at her phone as if that would suddenly make Gabriel call or text. Kirsten thought about telling Allison what happened as she set her phone down again and began getting her desk organized. After the last few days off, more than a couple things had found their way to her desk to be filed appropriately. On second thought, knowing Allison, she'd probably make it out to be something huge and act all dramatic about it. Best to wait until she had more information before telling her.

The day went by as usual, though significantly slower than Kirsten would have liked it to be. The hanging thoughts about Gabriel still weighed heavy on her mind. The workday came to a close, and with no word from Gabriel, Kirsten changed her mind and decided to text Allison about it once she got home. After changing and grabbing a snack, Kirsten sat down in her chair and texted Allison.

*'Hey, Allie, how are you?'* — *Kirsten*
*'I'm good. You ready for tomorrow?'* — *Allison*
*'Yea, I think so.'* — *Kirsten*
*'You think so?"* — *Allison*
*'Gabe had some trouble in Vegas.'* — *Kirsten*
*'Uh-oh, I'm calling you.'* — *Allison*

Kirsten rolled her eyes and immediately regretted sending any texts to Allison at all about it. She was still looking at her phone when Allison's call came through.

"Hello," Kirsten said as she put her phone on speaker and continued eating, hoping that she could make this conversation quick.

"Hey!" came Allison's voice from the other end. "So, what happened with Gabriel?"

Kirsten told Allison of the strange phone call from Gabriel and that she was worried about what and how it happened. "I'm probably just freaking out over nothing, honestly," Kirsten finished as she took the last bite of the food she had on her plate.

After a brief pause Allison finally spoke. "I wouldn't worry too much, girl. I'm sure everyone at the conference was held there for questioning."

"That's true," Kirsten agreed. "I'm hoping he can call soon and explain more."

"Same here. I'm sorry, girl. You'll hear from him soon, don't worry." Allison's voice came softer through the phone.

"Thank you," Kirsten said. "Have a good night, Allie. I'll talk to you tomorrow."

"You, too, Kirsten."

With that, Kirsten hung up the phone, cleaned up, and got ready for bed. Before Kirsten fell asleep, she sent a text to the unsaved number. She was subtly hoping they would offer some insight to the situation.

*'Is the weather okay?'* — *Kirsten*

*'Sunny as usual.'* — *Unknown*

*Strange*, Kirsten thought. If something was wrong, they would've informed her. However, since it seemed that everything was "as usual" then, she must not have anything to worry about. These thoughts stuck with Kirsten as she drifted off to sleep.

# Chapter 4

# Vegas

*A few days earlier.*

Gabriel woke up to the captain's message as they were coming into land. He glanced out the window of the plane next to his first-class seat. Gabriel could see the city of Vegas and the surrounding area. He had been here before and in several other places around the world. The view out the window on the descent into the airport was his favorite part, day or night. Looking out over the cityscape and seeing the various layouts and architecture, a small joy in his ever busy and demanding career.

Moments later, there was the familiar bump and squeal of the tires making contact with the pavement as the plane touched down. Gabriel collected his things once the aircraft reached the gate and headed through to the exit. His rental car was waiting for him as he left the terminal. While driving to his hotel, he thought about texting Kirsten that he'd arrived. This thought was short-lived, however, as a call came through his phone through the car.

*RING! RING! RING!*

The sound echoed through the car speakers, and the display showed Alex Thompson. "Hello," Gabriel answered.

"Well, I guess you landed safely then since you answered your phone." Alex's voice chuckled a bit as he spoke. Before Gabriel could respond, he continued, "I trust everything is in order for you there?"

"Yes, I'm pulling up to the hotel now," Gabriel said.

"Good," replied Alex. "I hope everything goes smoothly for you." He paused after speaking. Gabriel wasn't sure if he was done or waiting for a response. He had made sure everything was in order before he left back in Florida. Alex was back in Florida after a short stint in California working on closing another merger between another company on the west coast. Gabriel was here in Vegas to assist this merger so Alex shouldn't be concerned with anything at this time, especially since Gabriel had only just arrived in Vegas. His meeting hadn't even taken place yet. So, there was nothing to be speaking about now.

Alex continued after a moment, "I have been speaking to Allison." There it was. Gabriel knew that he wouldn't have called just to verify he made it safe to Vegas. Something else prompted this, and a conversation with Allison, that would do it. Allison had been a valuable member of the team for some time now. But lately, she had been acting irregularly, and it was creating a sense of uneasiness with other board members. There was talk of removing her, but that conversation was delicate because of the nature of her position and the business.

"Oh yeah? What does she have to say?" Gabriel said, his tone more sarcastic and annoyed than serious.

"She's getting reckless. I don't know how much longer we can trust her in her position," Alex explained.

"What is she saying now?" Gabriel asked. His tone grew more intense. He knew Allison was becoming a problem, but technically she didn't work for him, so he had left it alone. Gabriel was more concerned with focusing on Kirsten. He really couldn't care less about Allison at this point.

"She's threatening to reveal things before we are ready. She claims that she can handle more responsibility than we are giving her," Mr Thompson said. "I think she could be a problem." There was a weird seriousness to his tone. Gabriel wasn't sure what had just been happening, but he trusted Alex's feelings on the matter.

Gabriel agreed, "While she doesn't work for me directly, she is involved enough that maybe I can talk to her people and see what's going on and perhaps push it down the chain a bit. Clawing for more responsibility like this doesn't make me want to promote her, in fact, the opposite." Alex agreed and said he'd let the others know, and when Gabriel got back from Vegas, they would re-address the issue.

Gabriel checked into his room and unpacked. He didn't bring much since he was only going to be gone for a couple of days. There wasn't enough time on this trip to sightsee, just business, which made packing easy. Gabriel's phone notified him of the upcoming meeting and location, and after a quick shower and clothing change, he was off.

Gabriel headed to the conference center of the hotel. Inside and outside the room were several men in business dress socializing. Gabriel interacted briefly with a few of them before entering the room and finding his seat at the table. After a few minutes, the first meeting began. That meeting would last an hour, and after a short break, there was another.

Towards the end, Gabriel met with his contact Jeffery Thomas. He was set to be part of a big company merger between Gabriel's southeast coast operation and his southwest coast business. "Mr Ramirez," said a voice from behind. Gabriel turned quickly as he was waiting in the break area.

"Mr Thomas," Gabriel said as they met and shook hands. Jeffery Thomas, or Jeff, was the same height as Gabriel, though slightly plump around the midsection. He had a full head of dark hair with some greys above the ears. He was sporting a light button-down and slacks, as was his typical business casual. Gabriel wore something similar but looked less touristy with the color and style options. The two men started discussing the basics of the merge until the next meeting started. Once that meeting was done, they continued to talk.

"I just don't see how this gives me a profit," Jeff said as he and Gabriel left the conference area. Jeff had been less than receptive about this merger once they got into the details of what he would be getting with it.

Gabriel stopped him as he turned to face Jeff before speaking. "Let me show you the numbers over dinner," he said casually. Jeff agreed, and they headed to the restaurant in the same hotel. The restaurant was fairly busy and had a sense of modern luxury about it. Once seated, the men started talking business. Gabriel pulled out his tablet from the bag he had and swiped across the screen to pull up some of the info he needed.

Gabriel turned the tablet to show Jeff the spreadsheet. "Twenty percent," Gabriel started to say. To which Jeffery was about to immediately protest when the waitress came. After giving their order, Gabriel continued, "Twenty percent of all goods shipped and received. Additionally, all trade fees will be covered by my company, and you will still get ten percent of all distribution out of the west coast from your docks."

Jeff was not pleased nor convinced with this agreement and made it clear in his face. Gabriel reluctantly put the tablet away. "It's important to know that your refusal won't go over well with the others," Gabriel said.

Jeff leaned back in his chair. "Are you threatening me?"

Gabriel just shrugged and leaned back himself. "Not intentionally." He was calm and casual. Gabriel had had several conversations with various business deals in the past, and only a few of them were unsuccessful. Most had gone as one would think a typical business meeting would. A few, however, like this one, were less than desirable.

"Now you listen here," Jeff started to say. He leaned forward and continued, "I'm not stupid, I know exactly what kind of freight you're looking to move through my docks, and I won't take that risk for less than forty percent across the board."

Gabriel didn't move; he was used to this kind of conversation, and Jeff didn't threaten him. Not in the slightest. This merger was going to happen, one way or another. "Is that your final offer?" Gabriel asked.

"Yes."

"I will take your proposal to the others," Gabriel said. "We'll be in touch."

And with that, Gabriel got up, left some money and his business card on the table and walked away. Jeff sat in silence for a moment. He picked up the card and put it in his pocket and left money at the table with Gabriel's to cover the meal.

Once in his room, Gabriel called Mr Thompson. "Hey," he greeted when the phone connected.

"Did you make the deal?" Alex asked over the phone.

"He won't accept for less than forty percent across the board," Gabriel explained.

"I've already spoken to his board of directors. They are in line with our vision. If we can persuade or eliminate Jeffery Thomas, then the merger is guaranteed," Mr Thompson said.

Gabriel thought a moment before responding, "Is there a way to have him voted off the decision board?" he asked.

Alex was very concise as he spoke. "Not without inciting some very clear reason for a dismissal, which will most likely just bring our venture up to the forefront of the issue and the politics of the matter."

Gabriel sat quietly for a moment as he looked out his hotel room window. The sun was setting on the opposite side of the building from his room, and he gazed out over the sun-lit city. "Leave it to me. Perhaps I can... convince Jeff to retire of his own volition," he finally said.

"Very well. I'll leave it to you. Goodnight, Gabriel."

Gabriel hung up and sat on his bed. He had a few things that he could use, but they would take too much time to set up. He reached back for his phone and sent a text to an associate in his contact list. This then reminded him that he needed to text Kirsten and let her know he's okay. *"Later,"* he thought. He needed to meet with Jeff again before the last of the meetings tomorrow.

...*Later that evening*
*BANG! BANG! BANG!*

Gabriel awoke to the sound of pounding on his door. He took a minute to get the light and wake up a bit; meanwhile, the knocking continued.

*BANG! BANG! BANG!*

"Mr Ramirez," said a male voice from outside the room. "This is Officer Sloan, Vegas PD. I have a couple of questions for you."

Gabriel fumbled a response indicating he was coming. He looked at the clock and saw it was midnight. "Ugh," he muttered to himself as he got up and grabbed some pants.

Gabriel was only half-dressed as he opened the door as far as the chain lock would allow. Looking out, he saw the two men in police officer uniforms. The one who identified as Sloan, was standing closest to the door. "Yes," Gabriel asked questioningly.

"Mr Ramirez," Officer Sloan spoke again. "I'm Officer

Sloan, and this is Officer Smith. We are from the Vegas Police Department. We have some questions for you."

Gabriel nodded in response. "Mr Ramirez, do you know a Mr Jeffery Thomas?" Sloan asked, glancing down at his notebook.

Gabriel was calm and collected now. "I do, somewhat."

"When did you last see him?"

"Yesterday. We were at the same conference and met in person there," Gabriel began. "Afterward, we met for dinner here in the hotel and then parted ways after that. Why? What happened?"

Officer Sloan finished taking notes and then responded, "Jeffery Thomas was found dead tonight." Gabriel's face changed to concern as Sloan continued, "We found your business card in his belongings and based on what we know so far with what you've told us, you were the last person to see him alive."

"Oh."

"Yes, sir. Would you mind coming down to the station with us to answer some more questions?" Officer Sloan asked.

"Oh," Gabriel started. "Of course, let me just get dressed, and I'll need to call my lawyer and my girlfriend."

Officer Sloan nodded as Gabriel closed and unlatched the chain on the door. Officer Sloan carefully stepped in as Gabriel grabbed his shoes, shirt, wallet and phone before following the officers out.

# Chapter 5

# Night Out

Saturdays were usually slow starting for Kirsten, since that was her day to relax. This particular Saturday, however, seemed slower than usual. Kirsten had been up most of the night still going over the previous events. When she did finally sleep it wasn't very restful.

Before she knew it, Kirsten started to see the light of the morning sun coming through her window. Kirsten tried to avoid the light by rolling over and covering her head; however, even staying in bed longer than expected for her didn't help. It was about mid-morning when Kirsten finally gave in and got up.

Kirsten thought about canceling her plans with Allison that evening; however, she knew Allison would just find a way to make her go anyway. Not long after Kirsten was finally out of bed, she received a text from Allison.

'Hey, girl! I'm on my way over.' — *Allison*

'Okay, I'm just getting my day started. Had a rough night.' — *Kirsten*

'Understandable. See you in a few.' — *Allison*

Allison arrived at Kirsten's house around lunch. Kirsten was only half-dressed when she answered the door to let Allison in. As Allison came in, Kirsten noticed that Allison carried what looked like half of her closet and make-up drawer. After helping Allison get her stuff in and situated, Kirsten headed to the bathroom to finish cleaning up.

Allison had brought various styles of what she referred to as her "dancing clothes". These outfits ranged from an assortment of jeans with different tops and shoes to match; as well as a handful of dresses. Additionally, Allison had her backpack which carried her box full of accessories and make-up bag.

"Hey," Allison said somberly as Kirsten made her way to the bathroom. "Are you doing okay?"

"Yeah," replied Kirsten as she stepped into the bathroom, leaving the door open to still engage in the conversation. "It'll be okay. I've pushed Gabriel out of my mind till I hear more. No sense in worrying yet."

"True," said Allison. "Besides, I brought lunch. Plus, I need you in the best mindset so we can enjoy tonight."

"Speaking of which," Kirsten pipped up, poking her head out of her bathroom door. "What exactly is on the agenda tonight? I see you've brought a few things to try on."

"Ha-ha. Yes. We are going to that 'Magic 8' club just outside of town again," Allison responded playfully as she sorted through her things on the couch.

"Ugh," Kirsten replied as she rolled her eyes and pulled herself back into the bathroom.

Allison shot Kirsten a questioning glance. "What?" she said, trying to hold back her laughter, knowing full well what Kirsten meant in her response.

"You know what," Kirsten snapped mockingly, leaning back out of the bathroom door.

"Just because you almost went home with some guy because you were too drunk to care the last time we went," Allison began, no longer able to control her laughter.

What Kirsten was referring to was one of the first times that she and Allison went out together before she met Gabriel. It was during this night that the true bond of their friendship was tested as both girls got more drunk than usual and what started as harmless flirting for Kirsten became more troublesome as the recipient of her flirtatious behavior took it too far and tried to leave with Kirsten. Being significantly more intoxicated than she usually got, Kirsten had trouble both consciously saying no, as well as even wanting to say no.

Allison, though just as drunk, managed to retain some sense of sanity, enough to intervene (albeit at the last second) and managed to convince Kirsten to stay with her and avoid a drunken mistake, that in hindsight, may have ended her life based on what she was able to remember about the man she had been flirting with.

The girls were no stranger to guys hitting on them, and were also normally good about keeping each other from getting to the "too drunk to remember" point. Initially, this incident had turned Kirsten off to the idea that she should be hanging out with Allison under those circumstances. However, even then, Allison pulled through for Kirsten, so she got over it easily.

"Yes!" Kirsten quickly cut Allison off as she finished up in the bathroom and came out. "Because it wasn't safe. I have enjoyed every other girls' night we had, except that one."

"You'll be fine," Allison said, pretending to be annoyed. "We will keep to our normal routine as we have been," she finished.

"Should we do casual, or fancy tonight?" Allison asked as she was going through her clothes.

"If we are going to the Magic 8 club, we should probably look like we belong there a little bit," Kirsten said.

"True," Allison agreed. "I've got a new dress I've been

waiting to try." Allison pulled up a dress out of her bag. "Fancy it is."

Kirsten rolled her eyes as she turned to head into her room. "Of course you do." The girls ate a late lunch and continued to get ready throughout the afternoon. This time, time was spent doing more talking than actual dressing. Towards the evening the girls did some "pre-gaming" drinks before they finally left Kirsten's place.

Once the girls were ready, they headed out for the evening. Allison was wearing an attractive black dress that was somewhat fitted and cut off at the mid-thigh. The back was completely open and laced together from the shoulders to the tail bone, which tapered into a tight "V" shape that revealed the very top of her gluteal cleft.

The front came over in thin straps to a low-cut form that similarly matched the back, as it was open and laced from top to bottom. The dress gave full coverage of Allison's breasts, but the center was exposed as the laces went down the front and stopped in the same "V" shape just past her navel. Allison's make-up was heavy around the eyes but still reasonable overall. Together the outfit looked good, especially with Allison's choice of short thick wedge heels and a red necklace with a matching clutch.

Kirsten wore a soft red dress fitted to the hips with a decorative black belt around the waist and then flared out a bit to allow more smooth movement. The dress was longer on the right side, reaching just past her knees. From there, it tapered up towards the left and stopped mid-thigh. Kirsten's dress was a little more modest, as the dress had a solid back and front with some slightly poufy shoulder straps that were loose enough to fall down over her shoulders, which is where Kirsten preferred them anyway.

The dress's front thoroughly covered Kirsten's chest and met the shoulder straps that now hung around her upper arms; this worked well with the necklace she wore, a decorative gold chain with various colored stones throughout it. Kirsten kept her make-up more natural in appearance, except for her eyes, which she combined a red shadow with jet-black liner. Strapped sharp heels and her pocket wallet hanging from her wrist completed her ensemble.

"Should we eat beforehand?" Allison asked as they got into her car.

"Probably a good idea," Kirsten replied. "It's better to have something in my stomach before we add more drinks and the dancing."

"True that," Allison said as she started driving. "We should check out the new restaurant they added to the building."

"Definitely."

It was just after eight p.m. when the girls arrived at the club. It was an excellent establishment, just far enough out of town that it had enough room around it. So it didn't seem so crowded and helped with the ease of access with parking. As Allison said, it did have a new restaurant attached on one side, with the dance club on the other. LED lights all over, and a massive "8" pool ball from the game was dead in the middle between the two entrances. 'The Magic 8' was displayed in LED lights over the giant eight ball.

Allison pulled in and parked towards the center of the lot between the two entrances. It was early yet before the usual crowd would show up; however, the parking lot was still pretty full thanks to the restaurant that was now available. As the girls walked in, the atmosphere was calm and quiet. The girls were shocked that despite being next to the club, the music from there wasn't heard in dining area. The music that was heard, was a soft classical music that just filled the background. The servers and staff and all in attendance were well dressed, and the layout of the tables and décor gave it a modern and fancy look.

"Welcome, ladies," said the gentleman host at the front counter. "Just yourselves this evening? Or are you expecting company?"

"Just us," Allison stated.

"Excellent," replied the host. "Are you here just for dinner, or will you be attending the club later?"

"Both," Allison confirmed.

"All right, I'll just need to see some IDs then," said the host as he grabbed some papers from under the counter. "Is this your first time here with us?" he asked.

"The restaurant yes, but we've been to the club before," Kirsten replied as she reached for her ID.

The girls showed their licenses to the man. "Very good," he said. After reviewing them, the host grabbed some menus and pulled out a stamp pad from under the counter.

"As you might be aware then, no photography is permitted in the club area outside of the marked spot that is labeled as such." The host continued, "Please give me your right hands." The girls held their hands out, and he gently stamped the back of each one with an ultraviolet stamp. He went on to explain what the restaurant had to offer.

"This way, ladies," he said as he started to escort them towards a table. "All drinks purchased on the club side must stay on that side. There are restrooms both here, in the restaurant, and the club. Smoking is not permitted within the building. If you need to, you may use either of the main entrances and step outside to our designated smoking spots and simply show your hand to either myself here or the door guard on the club side to get back in."

They reached the table as he finished, and the girls sat down and began to browse the menu.

"Your server will be with you shortly," the host stated as he walked away.

As the host left, the girls talked about the plans for the night or, at least, attempted to. Allison's gaze kept wandering back towards the front. It was relatively easy for her since she sat facing that way at the table. Kirsten finally shot Allison an annoying glance. "Are you done?" Kirsten started to ask.

"What?" Allison responded, somewhat defensive. "He's gorgeous and…"

"Yes, I admit he's handsome, but we've got plans tonight," Kirsten interjected. "If you're that concerned, go get his number and set up something for later."

Kirsten was chuckling as she finished, but Allison called her bluff, left the table abruptly, and walked towards the front. Kirsten shouldn't have been surprised; Allison was very bold when it came to approaching men, but to her credit, she was also very good at it. In the past, Kirsten had mentioned that at some point Allison's behavior like that might get her in trouble, kidnapped, or worse, possibly even killed. Allison of course shrugged it off, because so far, she hadn't had any issues with it, and she would boast that she had "excellent taste."

Kirsten glanced behind her and watched as Allison very confidently approached the host. The front door was too far out of earshot, so Kirsten couldn't make out what Allison and the gentleman were conversing about; however, based on Allison's facial expressions, Kirsten could tell it wasn't going very smoothly.

Allison's return to the table was less chipper.

"So? How did it go?" asked Kirsten as Allison sat back down across from her.

"He's taken."

Kirsten gave a sarcastic sad face. "Pity."

Before they could talk further, the waitress approached the girls' table. The girls placed their order and began discussing some possibilities with Gabriel's absence again. Kirsten noticed that even though Allison was pretty engaged in the conversation, she seemed distracted. At first, Kirsten thought this was just due to the recent letdown; however, it appeared that Allison was continually glancing at her phone while the girls sat at their table.

It wasn't always super noticeable, but Allison would try to use her eyes and her head's natural movement to glance at her phone on the edge of the table. When the food arrived, Kirsten shook off the thoughts about what may have been troubling Allison, and the girls ate, enjoyed some more drinks and continued conversations about everyday items. It was almost ten when the ladies finished their meal and made their way to the club side.

As the girls walked through the short hallway, here they could faintly hear the music and see the faint light reflecting through the cracks around the door. The girls approached the double doors; the two burly men who had been sitting at the desk off to the girls' right, got up and motioned the girls to pause before entering.

"Hold up your right hands," said one of the men as he held up a small flashlight.

The girls casually did what they were told. The man waved the flashlight over their hands. It shone with a black-light and revealed the stamp on each of them. Meanwhile, the other bouncer very gently grabbed the ladies' left arms, raised them parallel to the floor, and did a quick pat-down around their midsection. Once the bouncer was finished, he nodded to the other, and they stepped aside and allowed the ladies to enter.

The club side was very spacious. Black-lights and LED

strips were everywhere. Immediately to their right was the bar, a large counter wrapped around the whole back corner of the area. In front of that was a seating area with small tables and chairs. Set up for those who wished to sit and enjoy the music rather than dance. To the girls' left was the club entrance to the outside. Two similarly stocky men were fleecing those who sought entry through that door.

A new feature, that wasn't there the last time the girls were, was the women in metal cages dancing on their own around the dance floor's outer edge. The pens, Kirsten thought, were probably to protect the dancers. This thought wouldn't take long to be confirmed as the girls headed through the seating area.

One of the dancers was in the process of swapping out with another dancer as some drunk idiot tried to jump in with her. The dancer screamed as a bouncer was already on his way from the back of the club and quickly grabbed the man and — very roughly — escorted him outside. Kirsten and Allison glanced at each other and looked around. No one seemed phased by the recent event.

The girls walked in further and shuffled around the people. The main crowd was growing and the dance floor was filling up. The stage at the end of the dance floor had a DJ in the center and other female dancers to each side of him.

The place overall was relatively full, considering the party hour was still approaching. Dance clubs didn't usually get super busy till later in the evening around there. The girls went out and danced for a bit, letting themselves loose for a few songs before heading back to the bar area.

"What is this?" Kirsten asked as Allison handed her a glass of what appeared to be a random mixed drink she had just gotten from the bar.

"A new drink for you to try," Allison responded playfully.

Kirsten shot her a sarcastic curious look and left the glass on the table in front of her. Allison was very quickly drinking hers until she noticed Kirsten wasn't partaking.

"Try it! It's good, you'll like it," Allison said reassuringly.

Kirsten took a sip as she still cast a suspicious smile at Allison. The drink was surprisingly smooth and delicious. Kirsten chuckled to herself as she drank more, making a mental note to ask Allison what it was.

"Hey, do you wanna go up on the balcony?" Allison suddenly said, glancing in that direction.

Kirsten looked over her shoulder towards the exit. There she saw a staircase that led to the balcony that went along the club's outer walls. Up on top were a few seating tables, pool tables, and a "Red Carpet" corner. A sign stating pictures were allowed in front of the corner with the red carpet and special lighting for those who wanted to pretend to be famous.

After a brief tour on the balcony and partaking in some photos in the red-carpet area, the girls went down to dance again as the club was quickly filling up at this point. After the ladies had been dancing for a bit, Allison's phone started vibrating with her camera light flashing. This feature was done by both girls to make sure they would notice their phones going off while dancing. Allison promptly pulled it out of her clutch and stared at the phone for a second.

"I'll be right back. Wait at the bar, and I'll meet you there when I get back," Allison said as she stepped away from the dance floor.

Kirsten watched as Allison left the dance floor and exited the club. Kirsten stood silent for a moment as the other people haphazardly danced around her. Kirsten made her way to the bar, as she did so, glitter and several other unknown substances were being thrown around the dance floor.

As Kirsten reached the bar, she couldn't help but feel abandoned. It wasn't like Allison to just walk out on her, even for a phone call. In all the times they have gone out together, it was Allison that made sure they always stuck together. Kirsten glanced around the club and immediately felt concerned for Allison's safety, as well as her own by herself. The more Kirsten thought about it, the more she felt she needed to follow up with it and followed Allison's path outside.

By the time Kirsten got outside, Allison was already out near her car. Kirsten made her way towards Allison's car making sure to keep a safe distance back and in her blind spot. Thankfully the parking lot was filling up with vehicles and people, so Kirsten found it relatively easy to stay hidden as she attempted to get closer to Allison's position.

Allison was already on her phone standing near her car facing away from the club. Kirsten was a few rows over, and as naturally as possible, walked around and very carefully approached Allison.

As she got closer Kirsten started to catch some of the conversation. "...of course I know," Allison snapped to whoever she was speaking to. There was a brief pause and Kirsten took a few more steps closer before hearing Allison again. "And you better do this for me or I'll blow this whole thing."

Kirsten froze for a moment; she glanced around and saw the staggering stream of people walking through the parking lot. Suddenly Allison turned. Not wanting to be seen, Kirsten crouched down and quickly walked through the cars nearby to get closer.

# Chapter 6

# Missing Pieces

Now in the next row over, Kirsten stayed crouched and pulled her phone out to pretend to look at it as she watched Allison. With the sounds from the club echoing outside and the crowd going in, Kirsten had a hard time hearing the whole conversation. It didn't help that she could only hear Allison's half.

"What happened?" Kirsten heard Allison say as she hid behind the other side of the vehicle. "That's ridiculous," Allison snapped after a few seconds of silence. "Of course, she doesn't know." Kirsten strained to listen further. "What time? ... Yea, I'll let her know and meet you there," Allison said faintly. Kirsten glanced up and peered through the car window and saw Allison walking back towards the club.

"Someone party too hard already?" Kirsten's heart jumped as she turned and looked up to see who was talking to her.

"Party too hard?" the voice repeated.

Kirsten quickly made her face look sick as she made eye contact with the gentleman standing there and nodded sheepishly as she stood up. Trying to make sure Allison wasn't still lingering around as she stood, Kirsten ran her fingers through her hair and pretended to put herself back together. "I'm good," Kirsten said to the man realizing how she must've looked to anyone who walked past the car while she was crouched there. "Must've been something I ate beforehand."

The man shrugged in acknowledgment and chuckled a little and continued to walk in with the couple friends he was with. Kirsten quickly turned and made her way back to the club trying to go slow enough to not cross paths with that stranger again, but also to be careful about being seen by Allison.

As she walked in Kirsten noticed that Allison wasn't at the bar. As she glanced around and didn't notice Allison in the crowd nearby initially, Kirsten hoped that Allison hadn't seen that she had just come from the entrance. Kirsten carefully made her way back inside and wandered the floor a bit as she looked for Allison.

The club was packed at this point, and moving about was becoming more difficult. Glitter and who knows what was being tossed around, the floor was sticky in some spots, and you were almost forced to touch everyone as you walked. Not that anyone there cared; people danced and as long as you didn't linger in their personal bubble uninvited, the crowd just ignored your presence.

As Kirsten made her way across to the dance floor and then around to the bar area. By the time Kirsten had made her way around, Allison was sitting at a table near the bar on her phone. "Hey, where'd you go?" Kirsten asked as she approached the table, trying to act as natural as possible.

Allison quickly laid her phone down screen first and smiled as she responded, "Took a call outside, but I've been back a while now. Where have you been? It looks like you've had some fun."

"What do you mean?" Kirsten questioned.

"You've got glitter, and who knows what else all over you," Allison said, chuckling to herself.

"Oh. Must've been while I was walking off the dance floor," Kirsten said as she glanced down at herself and pulled her hair in front of her face. She already knew what she looked like, after walking through the dance floor, but she played along to keep any doubts out of Allison's mind.

"What was the call about?" Kirsten asked as she attempted to brush off the glitter mess all over her.

"Nothing important," Allison responded. "But I will have to leave here sooner than expected."

"Oh?"

"Don't worry about it," Allison said as she got up and started to pull Kirsten to the dance floor. "Let's dance!"

The girls made their way back to the dance floor and began to relax a bit and enjoy the night. Allison took advantage of her revealing dress and let almost every guy grind up on her. Kirsten spent most of the time dancing either with Allison or on her own. She occasionally let a guy dance with her but wasn't as open about it as Allison appeared to be.

After some time and several more drinks, Allison motioned to Kirsten to follow her. Kirsten did and followed Allison off the dance floor and outside to the parking lot. It was after midnight now, and the girls laughed and talked about the evening as they got in Allison's car and headed back home. Both women were more intoxicated than they wanted to be. "Maybe I should drive," Kirsten said, almost as a question.

Allison just laughed in response, her chuckle was interrupted by a hiccup which made Allison reach for her chest and laugh more. "No, no," she finally said when she caught her breath. By now Kirsten was leaning on Allison's car and laughing with her. "I'll drive, you have too much to lose if we're pulled over. And I don't want to be the reason your career is lost." Kirsten conceded and sat in the passenger seat.

Kirsten just sat quiet on the ride home. Allison had some music playing, and was fairly smooth despite having so much to drink. *Too much to lose... my career is lost.* What did she mean by that? Kirsten's thoughts were a blur since she herself was also wasted. But what she could focus on didn't make sense. Perhaps it was just because Kirsten's drunk brain couldn't focus, or perhaps Allison misspoke through her drunk brain. Either way, it was strange.

After Allison dropped off Kirsten at her apartment, she headed home. Kirsten made her way inside her apartment and crashed on the couch. She was still unsure about Allison; however, she was too drunk to do anything about it tonight herself. Kirsten instead texted the unknown number to see if they could help.

*'Can you track Allison?'* — Kirsten

After a few minutes the response came.

*'Possibly. Why?'* — Unknown

*'She's drunk and acting strange after a phone call she got tonight.'* — Kirsten

*'Phone location shows she's almost home.'* — Unknown

"Damn," Kirsten said to herself.

Kirsten sat quietly for a moment. She noticed her feet were starting to hurt from her shoes, and glitter was now all over her couch. Perhaps she could get Allison to talk about what happened later. And with that, Kirsten faded out.

Kirsten awoke to her phone text alarm going off. After several minutes of trying to wake herself up, she looked at her phone; it was Gabriel!

*'Hey, babe, I'm back in town, and all is well. Let me know when you're available so we can get together.'* — Gabriel

Kirsten was both excited and annoyed and thought about not responding to avoid the drama of what was most likely to happen. But she knew she couldn't ignore him.

*'Hey, babe. Nothing is going on today. Otherwise, my work schedule is the same as always this week.' — Kirsten*

Kirsten got herself up still in last night's attire, and began to get ready for the day. After a hot shower and some coffee, Kirsten started to feel better. As the morning went on, she thought more about Allison's strange behavior. But these thoughts were quickly ridden of with the text from Gabriel. Kirsten was so excited to see him she could hardly stand it. Additionally, to finally hear about what happened in Vegas, it was something she was really looking forward to.

Kirsten was cleaning her house as she usually did on Sundays. And after managing to eat something for lunch, she texted Gabriel again to see when he was going to be available.

*'Hey, babe. When did you want to get together?' — Kirsten*

She didn't get an immediate response, but she didn't expect one either. Kirsten texted Allison next.

*'Hey, girl. What are you up to today? How are you doing?' — Kirsten*

Again, Kirsten did not expect nor did she receive an immediate response. Kirsten went and cleaned out her car to kill some time while she waited. Afterwards, Kirsten decided to go to the gym now that the hangover was gone.

Later that evening, while Kirsten was eating dinner and getting things ready for work, she got a text from the unknown number she had been communicating with:

*'Weather looks rough tonight.' — Unknown*
*'Hopefully, it'll clear up before morning.' — Kirsten*
*'North shipping yard, warehouse nine.' — Unknown*
*'Eleven p.m., recon only.' — Unknown*

Kirsten didn't respond; she didn't need to. It was only seven p.m. now. It was going to be a long night. Hopefully, she could still function for work tomorrow.

Still, no response from Gabriel or Allison as Kirsten got herself put together. Kirsten prepared to leave. Changing into dark pants and a shirt with comfortable dark shoes, she headed out.

As Kirsten got to her car, her phone buzzed, and she quickly checked it. It was Gabriel!

*'Hey, babe.'* — *Gabriel*

*'Do you want to get together tonight?'* — *Gabriel*

Kirsten had planned on scoping out the warehouse beforehand but decided that she should give Gabriel the chance to explain himself a bit about Vegas.

*'Sure. Where did you want to meet?'* — *Kirsten*

*'We can meet at your house. I'm near there anyway.'* — *Gabriel*

*'Okay, I'll be here.'* — *Kirsten*

Kirsten headed back inside, changed quickly, and waited for Gabriel to show up. Kirsten wouldn't have to wait long. Gabriel showed up about twenty minutes later, and he and Kirsten sat in her living room while Gabriel explained.

"How did this happen?" Kirsten asked after they had settled in.

"It's almost too crazy to be true," Gabriel responded.

"Try me," Kirsten snapped in a betting tone. She wasn't really mad, but Kirsten liked seeing Gabriel on edge right now in light of what happened.

Gabriel explained that one of the gentlemen at his work conference was found dead with Gabriel's business card in his pocket, so initially, he was just brought in for questioning with the others in attendance. However, after the initial interview, more evidence came up that made it seem more like Gabriel was the last to see the man before he died. Unfortunately, Gabriel didn't have an alibi that truly cleared him at first.

"After I called you and my lawyer, things started to look up as they dug deeper into the case," Gabriel continued. "Ultimately, it was found to be a random mugging, and I was cleared and allowed to leave."

"Strange, indeed," Kirsten said softly. "I was legitimately worried."

"I'm know. I'm sorry."

Kirsten moved closer and cuddled Gabriel. "Why didn't you call me to say you were coming home?"

"It was super late and I just wanted to finally be home," Gabriel explained softly.

The two continued to talk and catch up; Kirsten told Gabriel about the girls' outing last night. Gabriel agreed that Allison's behavior was strange, but seemed convinced it was the alcohol talking. After some time, the two made their way into Kirsten's bedroom and finished out the night there.

The next morning, Kirsten awoke first to her alarm. As she got up, she checked her phone and saw that she'd missed a text from the night prior.

*'Was the weather okay last night?'* — Unknown

"Shit," Kirsten muttered under her breath softly.

"What is it?" Gabriel asked as he touched her bare back from the other side of the bed.

"I might be late for work," Kirsten responded quickly as she got up to head to the bathroom.

"Not if we shower together," Gabriel responded, raising an eyebrow questioningly. Kirsten glanced back at him, gave a soft smile, and nodded for him to follow her. Gabriel practically jumped up to follow her to the bathroom.

Later that morning, Kirsten was at work when that same number texted again.

'*Amy's Diner, noon.*' — *Unknown*

'*Okay.*' — *Kirsten*

Kirsten knew she'd have to explain what happened last night. She wasn't overly concerned in the long run; however, right now, she wasn't sure about how to work this out.

# Chapter 7

# Mr Fox

Kirsten arrived at the diner a few minutes before noon. Amy's was a small diner closer to the edge of town. It had a very country, small-town feel as you walked in. Old style booths along the wall, a bar counter with stools near the kitchen window, and country décor throughout. Kirsten had known about the place already but had never been inside it until now. Glancing around the dining room as she walked in, Kirsten noticed that the place was pretty full, and she wondered how she would know whom she was meeting.

Just as Kirsten got a few steps in, the hostess came up and greeted her.

"Hello, how are you today, honey?" the hostess asked.

"I'm good, ma'am, thank you," Kirsten responded.

"Are you by yourself or with someone?"

"Meeting someone actually, but I'm not sure if they are here yet or not."

"Oh, right this way, sweetie."

Puzzled, Kirsten followed the hostess to a table against the far wall. The windows on the side of the building stopped just before this booth, leaving it lit only by the light above and somewhat secluded.

As they approached the table, Kirsten noticed a man sitting there already. He looked to be middle-aged man with dark skin.

The man was well-built and looked like he took care of himself. He wore a casual suit and had short buzzed hair. The grey hair color around his ears was the only way you could assume his age. The man was reading something on his phone as the hostess walked up.

"Excuse me, sir," the hostess said.

"Yes, what's up?" the man stated as he glanced up at the hostess. His response was firm but polite in his tone.

"I believe your guest has arrived."

The man looked over at Kirsten, took a glance up and down.

"Ms Jones," he said.

"Yes," Kirsten said quickly, not sure if it was a question or statement.

"Have a seat," the man said as he repositioned himself in the booth. Turning to the hostess, the man gave her his thanks and asked her to let the waitress know they were ready to order. Kirsten sat down carefully and somewhat rigid as she faced the gentleman.

"We've been corresponding for some time," the man said. Kirsten nodded slowly as he continued. "I thought this time we meet, perhaps then you'd feel better about the tasks assigned to you. I had rather hoped that this wouldn't be necessary, but your lack of response to last night created some... problems."

"It won't happen again," Kirsten cut in quietly. "I..." Her words trailed off as the waitress came up to the table. Kirsten and the man both ordered just sandwiches and water. Once the waitress was out of earshot, Kirsten continued.

"I promise it won't happen again. I had an unexpected visitor last night."

"Yes, I'm aware."

Kirsten tried to hide the initial shock on her face, but the man caught it.

"What? Did you think the text messages were the only way I communicate and keep tabs on you?" the man asked redundantly.

"I suppose not," Kirsten said. Now slightly annoyed and concerned about whether or not she has a secret stalker, or worse, hidden cameras she didn't know about in her place.

"Thankfully, another opportunity has come up. Same warehouse, same time, this coming Friday night," the man said.

The man explained a few details about the upcoming event, stating that it would be just a recon trip to gain information about the activity and conversations heard, if possible, that would be happening there. As he finished, the waitress came with their food. Kirsten wasn't hungry, but she forced herself to eat.

After they finished eating, Kirsten grabbed her purse, but the man stopped her and said he'd pay for the meal. Grateful, but feeling awkward again, Kirsten got up to leave. Before she stepped away from the table, she turned back and asked for his name.

"What, are you going to put me in your contact list?" the man responded, chuckling. "No, my number changes too much to be concerned with that; however, since we will be working together for some time yet, you may call me Mr Fox." Kirsten partially rolled her eyes as she turned to walk away.

"Finish this, and you'll be done for a while," Mr Fox said quickly. Kirsten paused, then continued to leave the restaurant.

Work the rest of the day dragged on as Kirsten thought more about her lunchtime meeting. Before work ended, Kirsten texted Allison again to see what was going on with her. The two of them have been friends since before Kirsten starting seeing Gabriel, and they had grown very close in that time-frame.

Both Allison and Kirsten had similar interests and backgrounds, and in the time they knew each other, they had shared a lot of their personal stories. This friendship they had, made it all the stranger for Allison's recent behavior and distancing. Today, however, Allison responded to Kirsten's text right away as usual.

'Hey, girl.' — *Allison*
'Hey, Alli. How are you doing?' — *Kirsten*
'Pretty good. Just working. You?' — *Allison*
'Same. Did you want to hang out tonight?' — *Kirsten*
'Sure. What time? I don't get off work till five p.m.' — *Allison*
'Probably around seven-thirty p.m. I'm gonna go to the gym.' — *Kirsten*
'That works for me. I'll text you when I'm on my way. See you then.' — *Allison*

After work, Kirsten hit the gym and headed home. Afterward, Kirsten felt better about the events that were going on and talking to Allison. Getting back to her routine and taking some stress out through these activities helped.

Once home, Kirsten showered quickly, heated some leftovers, and checked her phone. Gabriel had texted while she was in the shower, so she needed to respond to that.

'Hey, babe. Sorry I didn't respond sooner. I was in the shower.' — *Kirsten*
'No worries. How was your day?' — *Gabriel*
'Not bad. How was yours?' — *Kirsten*
'Pretty good. I have a meeting tonight. But if you want, we can try and get together tomorrow.' — *Gabriel*
'Sure!' — *Kirsten*
'I love you.' — *Gabriel*
'I love you, too.' — *Kirsten*

It was just after seven p.m. when Allison texted saying she was on her way, and around seven-thirty p.m., Allison texted she was on her way up to the apartment. Kirsten unlocked her door and greeted Allison when she walked up a few minutes later.

"Hey, how have you been?" Kirsten asked as they hugged.

"I'm good — been busy lately with work," Allison replied as she very comfortably fell into Kirsten's couch.

"It seems like it," Kirsten said, half chuckling as they sat down in the living room. "So, what happened last weekend?"

"Part of it was work, part of it was boys," Allison said.

Allison explained that since she deals in the shipping department of the firm she works at and was on call that weekend, she was tasked with correcting some shipping issues with the manifests. Additionally, Allison disclosed she had been talking to a guy for a little while now. Although they hadn't labeled themselves, it had been getting closer to an actual relationship.

The two girls continued to talk for some time about their personal lives and what'd been going on. Kirsten explained more about what happened with Gabriel and told Allison what Gabe had told her about his trip to Vegas. After a couple of hours and some wine, the girls decided it was time to call it a night.

The rest of the week went by just fine. Kirsten and Gabriel spent a few nights together over the next few days, and things were looking good for them in the coming days ahead.

That Friday, Kirsten went to work as usual and set up her plans for that evening and how she would scope out the warehouse. Kirsten got home, changed, ate, and got ready to head out. She had already told both Gabriel and Allison that she wouldn't be available that evening using her go-to excuse that she would be going to the gym and then wanted a quiet night to herself.

It was around eight p.m. when Kirsten arrived at the warehouse. Initially, Kirsten drove past and around the surrounding area; to get the layout of the site before it got too dark. This particular shipping yard was relatively small comparatively and only had occasional patrols. Shipping containers and various warehouses were staged throughout. A few stadium lights staggered around gave some light as the sun went down but left enough shadows to help with concealment.

To avoid suspicion, Kirsten parked her car near others at a building that was some distance away from the warehouse she was observing. Kirsten waited in her car for a few minutes until it was just after nine p.m., then made her way to warehouse nine.

Kirsten found a secluded spot behind some pallets near one of the nearby buildings. It was a little farther away than she would've liked, but it was probably better this way. From this distance, she would be better hidden. After some time with no movement around the building, Kirsten checked her phone: ten p.m.

"Ugh," Kirsten muttered softly as she rolled her eyes to herself. *They don't show this part about stakeouts in the crime shows and movies,* Kirsten thought, *this was going to be a long night.* After what seemed like forever, it was finally eleven p.m. Kirsten hadn't seen or noticed any movement around the warehouse up to this point and started to wonder if Mr Fox got his details mixed up. No sooner had Kirsten thought this when a vehicle pulled up outside the warehouse.

Kirsten got her phone out and used the camera to zoom in and get a better look. The license plate wasn't able to be seen very well because of the headlights, even from Kirsten's angled viewpoint across the way. Kirsten still took as many pictures as possible, trying to get the vehicle information and any faces of the people getting out.

Three men of average height and build exited the car and walked towards the warehouse. The fourth, the driver, pulled the car around the warehouse's side, and after turning off the vehicle, followed the others inside. Kirsten recognized some of the men as the ones that she was introduced to at the fundraiser where she met Gabriel. She didn't recognize the driver though, all she could make out was his clothing and general height and weight, but as she took the pictures, she hoped that Mr Fox would find something useful in them.

As another car approached, Kirsten noticed the approaching vehicle's headlights lit up the previous car just enough on the back to see the license plate. Kirsten quickly snapped a few shots of the rear end of the first car, then focused on the second car's occupants. Rather tall and slender, two men exited the vehicle with a female, who was short and slim. The men appeared to be wearing what looked like business casual clothes. The female was wearing dark pants and a jacket. Her hair was down and covered most of her face from Kirsten's angle.

The driver of the second car pulled his car up next to the other side of the building. As the driver got out, Kirsten was ready with her camera. The man walked under the light near the door, but before entering, glanced around behind him. Kirsten snapped a few photos to get as many as possible. As she did, she realized the man who just entered the warehouse looked a lot like Gabriel.

## Chapter 8

## New Information

Kirsten quickly went through the photos she took and sent the best shots to the unknown number she still had in her phone from her last correspondence with Mr Fox. Afterward, Kirsten took a minute to better look at the previous couple of shots she got of the man that looked like Gabriel.

Unfortunately, the photo didn't show enough detail to get a good look at his features and confirm her suspicions. However, Kirsten decided she would wait around to see if she could catch them coming out of the warehouse when they finished whatever they were doing in there.

*'Much appreciated.'* — *Mr Fox*

The text popped up a few minutes later. Kirsten ignored it as she glanced around the warehouse and wondered if she could get a view inside. There were no windows she could see, but after checking that no one was around to see her, she left her hiding spot and made her way closer. As she approached the warehouse, she noticed headlights in the distance headed towards her. Not sure if it was more company or the regular patrols, Kirsten ducked near the parked cars and carefully crept around them, staying out of the light.

The headlights drew closer as Kirsten waited. The air was getting cold, and she suddenly felt a chill run through her from the breeze off the water. The vehicle approached and continued past the warehouse and Kirsten's location. With a sigh of relief, Kirsten made her way around the cars, and using the light from the warehouse door, took better pictures of the license plates and sent them off to Mr Fox as well.

Trying not to attract attention, Kirsten used her phone light to make her way around the back of the warehouse. But to her disappointment, there was nothing; no windows, no doors, nothing. "Damn," Kirsten muttered to herself. Kirsten glanced at her phone; it was almost midnight now. Mr Fox never responded to her last texts with the license plate numbers and without knowing how long the people would be in there before they left, Kirsten made her way back to her hiding spot earlier and decided to wait a bit longer before calling it a night.

It was almost one a.m. when Kirsten finally made it back to her car and headed home. No one had left the warehouse, and since her instructions were 'recon only', Kirsten decided to leave. She still counted it as a win since she got some good pictures.

Running through the night's events, Kirsten made plans to herself to see Gabriel that weekend and see what he said, if anything. Once home, Kirsten showered to try and relax and then went straight to bed.

Kirsten woke up later that morning and texted Gabriel right away.

*'Hey, babe! How are you doing today? Did you want to hang out?'* — Kirsten

No immediate response. Kirsten got up, showered, and dressed. While she was eating, her phone text ding came through.

*'Hey, girl! Wanna hang out today?'* — Allison

*'Sure.'* — Kirsten

*'Gabe and I are working on getting together today; so I may have to cut our time short.'* — Kirsten

*'No worries.'* — *Allison*

About an hour later, Kirsten met Allison at an ice cream shop downtown.

"Hello! How are you?" Kirsten asked as she hugged Allison. She noticed that Allison looked drained and tired around the eyes, almost as if she'd been out all night.

Allison nodded her head and replied sheepishly, "I'm fine, just tired."

"I'll admit, you look a bit drained," Kirsten said.

"Yea, I had a long night," Allison said as they sat down at one of the tables outside the shop.

"Oh? Did anything interesting happen?" Kirsten asked playfully. She was sure Allison was about to disclose some dirty details about her new man. Unfortunately, this would not be the case. "Nothing much," was Allison's only response as she glanced at her phone before putting it back in her purse.

Kirsten nodded in acknowledgment and didn't push the issue. But throughout the conversation, Kirsten couldn't help but wonder what happened that kept Allison from telling her. Allison had never been shy about sharing the details about any romantic encounter, even if it was slightly embarrassing. Allison had no reason to lie to hide anything from Kirsten given the strength of their friendship, and if it was just a bad night for sleep, then Allison definitely should've been able to mention why. To keep any red flags from showing up, Kirsten didn't ask about last night further and also kept the conversation away from any mention of what she had been up to last night.

After about an hour or so, Kirsten got a text from Gabriel saying he was available anytime to meet up today. Allison and Kirsten said their goodbyes, and Kirsten headed to Gabriel's place. Kirsten loved going to Gabriel's place since their relationship started. The view, the condo, the beach — she enjoyed every minute spent there.

Gabriel greeted Kirsten as the elevator doors opened. Barefoot with white pants and an open white button-down shirt, Kirsten couldn't help but let her eyes give her away as she gazed up and down at Gabriel as she walked into the condo and his arms. Kirsten inhaled deep. The cedarwood and cinnamon scent was strong on Gabriel. It was Kirsten's favorite, and she made sure to tell him.

"Let me use the bathroom quick," Kirsten said, breaking off the make-out session that had just started.

"Of course," Gabriel said.

Kirsten headed for the bathroom; once there, she noticed a panty liner wrapper in the trash next to the toilet. The trash can was empty, save for a few tissue pieces and the wrapper. Kirsten brushed it off initially as a wrapper for something else, but after looking further, she realized it was, in fact, the wrapper to a panty liner.

Several thoughts raced through Kirsten's mind; perhaps Gabriel had a family or co-worker gathering, then it could easily have belonged to someone from those events. It also could be very old since it was just Gabriel here.

Kirsten tried to recall the last time she was in the condo, thinking perhaps it was hers. Kirsten didn't remember needing one at any of the times she'd been here. However, it could be possible that it was.

These thoughts and more swirled through Kirsten's brain quickly while she was in there. As she returned to Gabriel, Kirsten acted casual as she and Gabriel picked up where they left off. Of course, they weren't long into it before both of them found themselves in Gabriel's bedroom. Any concern for what Kirsten found was gone as she wrapped herself in Gabriel's affection.

*RING, RING, RING!*

The phone startled both Kirsten and Gabriel, both of whom had fallen asleep. Gabriel, still naked, rushed up and grabbed his phone from his pants pocket.

"Hello," Gabriel said, trying to sound as casual and normal as possible. Gabriel continued his conversation as he walked out of his room. Kirsten got up to get dressed and checked her phone. No missed texts or calls. Kirsten then saw the time was almost four-thirty p.m. She wasn't sure when she and Gabriel had finally relaxed enough to fall asleep. But based on how she felt, it seemed she got a good nap in. However, she noticed her head was aching again.

Kirsten grabbed her underwear and went to the bathroom to clean up. Once there, Kirsten remembered the wrapper in the trash and needed to ask Gabriel about it. Gabriel was still talking on the phone when Kirsten got out to the main room of the condo. Gabriel had slipped on some shorts now and was still talking to the person on the phone.

"Yes. Thank you. I'll be in shortly," Gabriel said as he motioned to Kirsten to wait. Gabriel hung up the phone and smiled at Kirsten as she walked closer playfully swaying her hips as she did. Gabriel smiled harder and took a step forward to meet her as she approached. "I'm sorry, love. I have to go to the office," Gabriel said as he pulled Kirsten in close.

"It's okay," Kirsten said as she kissed his cheek. "I do have a question, though." Her hands rest on his chest. His arms wrapped around her meeting together in the small of her back, holding tightly. Kirsten relaxed a bit; she loved the way she felt when he held her.

"Sure, what's up?"

"In your bathroom trash can, I saw a panty-liner wrapper. I'm just curious where it came from and how long it's been there," Kirsten asked softly. Try as she might, she couldn't keep the nervousness out of her voice.

Gabriel had a puzzled look. "I haven't used that bathroom in a while; I didn't even know." He paused, thinking about it before continuing. "It may have been my office assistant. She was here with a couple of the board members before I went to Vegas." Gabriel's eyes showed sincerity as he answered, and Kirsten gave him a loving kiss before she responded.

"I figured that's what it might have been, but I thought I'd ask just to be sure."

"I'll call you tomorrow," Gabriel said as he squeezed her tighter and kissed goodbye.

"For sure."

Kirsten left and headed home. Her thoughts swirled around the events of last night and this afternoon. In Kirsten's mind, if it was Gabriel she saw at the warehouse last night, then it brought up a bunch of other questions about Mr Fox and Gabriel. However, if it wasn't Gabriel, it was simply a curiosity about what was going on. On a separate note, Kirsten was concerned about Allison. It wasn't in her character to be so elusive to Kirsten about whatever goes on. Kirsten continued to ponder this information as she drove home.

After she got home, Kirsten decided she needed to relieve some stress, and changed, and went to the gym. Once there, Kirsten texted Allison to check in and see how she was.

*'Hey! I hope your day got better. I'm at the gym now, but if you want to talk, let me know.'* — *Kirsten*

Kirsten didn't expect an immediate response. However, she hoped Allison would reach out to her and fill her in on what's going on.

It was after seven p.m. when Kirsten left the gym and headed home. Allison never responded to Kirsten's text, but Kirsten wasn't too concerned yet. Kirsten tried calling Gabriel, but it went to voicemail. She hung up without leaving a message and texted him instead.

*'Hey, babe! Just got done at the gym, and I wanted to say goodnight and I love you.'* — *Kirsten*

Kirsten headed home, and though her thoughts were calmer after the workout, she still couldn't help herself from still thinking about the events and what Mr Fox is up to. As Kirsten got to her place, she parked her car and decided to take the stairs up to her apartment. Kirsten got to her door, unlocked it, walked in, and shut the door behind her.

"Ms Jones!" said a voice from a man inside her apartment. Kirsten screamed lightly and practically jumped out of her skin. "Good evening," the stranger continued. His voice was calm but firm. Kirsten was still coming down from her fright as she reached in her bag for her pepper spray. "You won't need that," the man said, still sitting calmly in the chair in her living room.

Kirsten frantically glanced up and realized who was there, though still partially concealed by the lack of light. Kirsten began to calm down as she started to recognize who it was… "Mr Fox," Kirsten said, somewhat annoyed now and still catching her breath. "I'd ask how you got in here, but at this point, it is irrelevant," Kirsten said as she sat down on her couch, facing him, and asked, "What are you here for?"

"I'm here to commend you on a job well done for Friday night. Your pictures proved most useful in our investigation," Mr Fox explained.

"Glad it wasn't for nothing," Kirsten responded.

"Indeed. I have a team looking into some of the leads from the license plates you sent me. And our tech guys are working on enhancing the photos of the individuals involved." Mr Fox continued. "We hope to have more info soon."

Kirsten sat down on her couch and faced Mr Fox. "Good. A few of them I recognized from a year ago, the night I met Gabriel at that fundraiser. They were there."

"Yes, we knew about those men already," Mr Fox said as he leaned forward. "The others now need to be identified." As he finished speaking, Mr Fox got up and started walking to the door. "Be careful," he said casually. Kirsten nodded slowly but didn't move otherwise and kept sitting the way she was. Mr Fox glanced back at her as he reached the door. "Hopefully, we get this done soon," he said.

Kirsten glanced over her shoulder looking at Mr Fox in the doorway and nodded again.

"Sorry for the scare," Mr Fox said as he left the apartment.

Once the door closed, Kirsten breathed a sigh of relief. After a moment, she got up, locked her door, and went to the shower. Kirsten stood there for several minutes, trying to get herself to relax by just letting the hot water run over her. As she finished, she cleaned up a bit and went to bed.

Sleep wouldn't come easy. Kirsten's mind raced around, and her nerves were still tense about her conversation with Mr Fox. Even though she and Mr Fox had interacted before and were working together, Kirsten was still shaken up a bit about finding him just sitting in her home. These thoughts and others ran through Kirsten's mind as she lay there trying to fall asleep.

Kirsten awoke the following day, still feeling tired and unsure when she finally fell asleep. She rolled out of bed and checked her phone. No new notifications, seven-thirty a.m.... "Ugh." Kirsten sighed as she rolled her eyes. She set her phone down and laid back down across her bed, contemplating if she even wanted to get up. After a few moments, Kirsten sat up and went to her kitchen to make coffee.

*RING, RING, RING!*

Kirsten had no sooner sat down to enjoy her coffee on this quiet Sunday morning when her phone started ringing from her bedroom. "Ugh," Kirsten sighed and rolled her eyes again as she got up to go get the phone.

*RING, RING, RING!*

Kirsten looked at the screen and quickly answered when she realized it was Allison calling. "Hey, Allie!" Kirsten greeted in the best chipper tone she could muster. "How are you?"

"I'm okay," Allison said. "Are you home? I need to talk to you."

"Yea, I got no plans today."

"Great, I'll swing by in a bit."

Kirsten hung up and tipped her head back in an exhausted, annoyed motion. Mustering up the energy, Kirsten drank some of the coffee that was still in her hands and then quickly threw herself together.

Approximately an hour later, Kirsten heard a knock at her door. Kirsten opened to see Allison, somewhat disheveled, standing there. Kirsten glanced up and down at Allison's appearance.

"What happened to you?" Kirsten asked, chuckling under her breath. "You look like you've been up partying all night." Allison only responded with a mocking, smug, half-smile and pushed past Kirsten and let herself in. "Okay," Kirsten said softly as she shut her door, and proceeded to sit down next to Allison on the couch.

"I'm sorry," said Allison after a moment of silence. "I've been up all night, thinking about how to process this and I'm just drained."

"It's okay," Kirsten replied. "What's going on?"

Allison took a deep breath to compose herself before finally saying, "You need to break up with Gabriel."

# Chapter 9

# Doubts

Kirsten sat speechless for a moment as dozens of thoughts raced through her head at once. She was frozen stiff; every memory flashed in her head in an instant. How did Allison know this? She introduced her to Gabriel, so why is this suddenly not okay? "What? What do you mean I need to break up with him?" Kirsten snapped, somewhat defiantly.

"You need to break up with Gabriel," Allison repeated, keeping her tone the same.

Kirsten's toned changed from concern to a silent anger as Allison finished. "Yes, I heard that part. Why?"

"I think he's cheating on you," Allison said solemnly. Her eyes darted away from Kirsten's as she spoke. She was afraid to look her in the eye. It was a hard conversation to have with Kirsten given how close they were, and it was her fault for bringing Kirsten and Gabriel together.

"You think?" Kirsten snapped. "What do you mean 'you think'?"

"I..."

"And how did you even find out?" Kirsten interrupted. "And who is he supposedly cheating on me with? When did he actually do it? How often?" Kirsten tried to retain her composure while still emphasizing to Allison the seriousness of her concern of these accusations. Gabriel had never hinted nor acted like he was cheating, and up until this conversation Kirsten didn't have any reason to doubt their relationship.

Allison waited calmly as Kirsten grilled her with questions. When Kirsten had quieted down, Allison went on to explain. "Kirsten, we've been friends for almost a year," Allison started to say. "I was able to introduce you to Gabriel thanks to mutual friends I had with him."

"I'm aware of this part," Kirsten said, starting to get annoyed at the delay in her questions being answered.

Allison ignored Kirsten's attitude and continued. "I was thrilled for you to meet Gabriel since all the things I heard about him were great."

"But?" Kirsten interjected.

"But through my interactions with these coworkers, they mentioned that Gabriel might be spending time with another woman," Allison finished.

"Might?" Kirsten snapped. "You don't know for sure?" Allison just shook her head. "Well, thanks for the doubts that will now haunt my thoughts over something that may or may not be happening," Kirsten said.

Allison and Kirsten sat quietly for a few moments before either spoke again. Kirsten started to process the possibility of what Allison just told her. Allison moved closer to Kirsten and put her arm around her. Kirsten leaned her head on Allison's shoulder and closed her eyes. As Kirsten sat there and continued thinking, Allison held tight and tried to give some comfort to Kirsten in silence.

Thoughts and questions raced through Kirsten's head as she started to question any delayed text or cancelled date — hypothetically playing out what could have been going on in those moments. *Who was this woman? How did Gabriel know* her? *What did she look like?"* All questions that Kirsten thought, then there was the panty liner in his trash. Did he lie about that?

Kirsten started to tear up a little. Allison brought up her other hand to Kirsten's face to wipe the tears and then gave her a hug. "As soon as I know more, I'll let you know," Allison said quietly. Kirsten nodded.

After a moment, Allison finally got up to leave. Kirsten didn't say anything more, and Allison took the hint based on Kirsten's body language that she needed to be alone. As Allison reached the door, she turned back to say goodbye. "I'm so sorry, Kirsten." Kirsten still looked down, and Allison just lowered her head and walked out.

After Allison left, Kirsten sat in silence for some time. Finally, after what seemed like forever, Kirsten shook off the thoughts and tears and forced herself to continue her day to help get her mind off things.

She texted Gabriel good morning and got herself dressed. Gabriel said he'd call today, and he'd never failed to communicate if the plans changed; however, with this new information, Kirsten's usual calm about it turned to anxiety the longer she waited without hearing from him.

Kirsten finally had an idea about how to calm herself and prove to Allison she was misinformed. Kirsten grabbed her phone and browsed her contacts.

*'I need your help.'* — *Kirsten*

After a few minutes, the reply came...

*'What do you need?'* — *Mr Fox*

*'You've been watching me, does that mean Gabriel is on your radar?'* — *Kirsten*

*'Possibly.'* — *Mr Fox*

*'Do you know, or can you find out if he's been cheating on*

*me?'* — *Kirsten*

No response. Kirsten waited for a bit before putting her phone down, but as she did, it started ringing. 'Mr Fox' ... Kirsten quickly answered.

"Hello," Kirsten greeted quietly.

"I'm not your personal, private detective," came Mr Fox's voice on the other end of the line.

"I'm aware of that," replied Kirsten. "But Allison seemed super convinced it's happening, and I'm at a loss on what to think. And how to move forward."

Mr Fox breathed heavily through the phone before responding.

"I will... see what I can find," Mr Fox said solemnly. "But I'm not going to waste a bunch of my time or the resources to do so."

"Thank you," Kirsten said.

"Enjoy the rest of your weekend, Ms Jones."

"I will try."

Kirsten hung up and felt a little better. There was no guarantee about what, if anything, Mr Fox would find. However, Kirsten felt some relief about the situation, knowing she would receive some answers.

Later that day, Kirsten was cleaning her apartment when her phone rang. When she got to it and saw who was calling, she about jumped in her skin: 'Gabriel'. Any relief that Kirsten had before was now gone faced with the reality that she would have to talk to him knowing what she knew now, at least, hypothetically.

Kirsten took a deep breath and answered the phone. "Hey, babe!" Kirsten said as chipper as possible.

"Hey," Gabriel responded. "Do you want to grab some

dinner?"

"Sure. What time?" Kirsten asked.

"Are you free in an hour?"

"Yep."

"Cool. I'll pick you up. See you soon."

"Okay," Kirsten said as she hung up the phone. She breathed deep but soft, trying to calm down before Gabriel showed up. Kirsten glanced at the clock; it was almost four p.m. Quickly, Kirsten finished what she was doing and changed her clothes. She was done before five p.m. and sat down in her living room browsing her phone until Gabriel showed up.

It was around a five-fifteen p.m. when he buzzed at the door. Kirsten immediately got up and let him in. Gabriel stood there with flowers and a hug. Whatever doubt Kirsten had, was gone. At that moment, she allowed herself to be swept up in Gabriel's arms, and as he planted a soft kiss on her lips, Kirsten melted. In her mind, she loved him. She thought about asking Gabriel about what Allison had said, but then reconsidered when she realized that it would cause unnecessary problems between the three of them until she could prove it.

After what seemed like forever, yet not long enough, Kirsten let herself down from her tiptoes and just stared into Gabriel's eyes. He smiled back as he asked if she was ready to go. Nodding quickly, Kirsten let go of Gabriel's neck and took the flowers and set them on her coffee table, grabbed her purse, which sat by the door, and then left with Gabriel, arm in arm.

The dinner went great as Kirsten and Gabriel made casual small talk. Kirsten avoided any topic that would lead to her thinking about what Allison said and cause her to ask Gabriel directly about it. Her strategy seemed to work well and the evening went on uneventful and very smoothly. Afterward,

Gabriel dropped off Kirsten back at her place and headed home. Kirsten, feeling exhausted, cleaned up and went to bed.

Monday morning came, and Kirsten went about her routine at work. Kirsten was eating lunch when her phone went off.

*'I have some information for you.'* — *Unknown*

At first, Kirsten was puzzled but then rolled her eyes to herself as she realized that Mr Fox must've changed his number again.

*'What did you find out?'* — *Kirsten*
*'I'll meet you tonight with everything I have.'* — *Mr Fox*
*'What time?'* — *Kirsten*
*'Seven p.m. Your place.'* — *Mr Fox*
*'Okay.'* — *Kirsten*

Kirsten changed the contact info in her phone so that the new number was updated. But now, the rest of the day would drag on. Kirsten was excited and nervous about getting the information. Thoughts raced through her mind as she re-read the texts.

Mr Fox didn't hint whether it was good or bad info. Which almost made it worse as Kirsten suspected that that meant it was terrible, and he didn't want her to worry until he was able to give the information to her directly.

Kirsten tried to keep the thoughts at bay and not worry about it. However, the afternoon still dragged on as she continued to work. Once work was over, Kirsten went to the gym and then home. She hadn't texted or spoken to Gabriel or Allison at all today. However, it was probably best that she wait until Mr Fox reveals his information.

As Kirsten sat on her couch, she glanced at her clock: six p.m. As Kirsten sat waiting for Mr Fox to call or arrive, her thoughts began to wander to memories with Gabriel. How perfect he acted when they met and how much of a gentleman he was…

The yacht party was terrific; string lights everywhere, men and women dressed in fancy clothes. Kirsten felt entirely underdressed for this event even though her plain and simple white dress was lovely. However, compared to the brand names and jewelry she was seeing around her, Kirsten still felt uncomfortable as she wandered through the crowd.

"Kirsten!" shouted a familiar voice from across the small crowd gathered on the upper level of the yacht.

"Allison," Kirsten answered happily as she made her way towards her.

"I'm so happy you made it," Allison said excitedly as Kirsten got closer and gave her a hug.

"I feel like I don't belong here," Kirsten replied as she glanced around and then back at herself.

"Nonsense!" Allison said. "You look amazing. Besides, Gabriel already likes you."

"Yea, but..."

"No buts," Allison interrupted. "Come on. He's waiting downstairs."

Before Kirsten could respond, Allison grabbed her hand and led her through the crowd. They went below into the main room of the yacht below. As the girls made their way down, Kirsten's nerves got the better of her, and she pulled back against Allison's lead. "What's the matter?" Allison asked.

"I don't know. I've only had the two dates with Gabriel, and they were great and I really like him, but I feel he's way out of my league," Kirsten responded softly. "I don't fit in with this crowd."

Kirsten was overtaken with emotion around Gabriel. Since Allison first introduced them, it'd been nothing but butterflies and flushed checks for Kirsten ever since. There was something about the way he spoke, the way he smelled, the way he moved that had Kirsten hooked, and she couldn't understand why.

"That's part of why he likes you," Allison responded, grabbing Kirsten's hand again, this time more softly, and led Kirsten the rest of the way. Gabriel was standing at the bar across the room from where the girls entered. His dark hair was perfectly groomed, and his sleek suit was nicely tailored to fit his toned physique better. To Kirsten, he stood out among the others around the yacht just by being in the room.

After seeing Gabriel, Kirsten softened her reluctance against Allison and more willingly picked up her pace walking towards him. When he noticed them, Gabriel excused himself from the men he was talking to and took a few steps in the girls' direction to meet them as they approached.

"Hello, ladies," Gabriel said calmly.

"Hey, Gabe," Allison said quickly.

Gabriel turned to Kirsten, who flushed a little when their eyes met. Allison immediately let go of Kirsten's hand and let out a small chuckle. Kirsten was lost in Gabriel's eyes as he gently grabbed her right hand and brought it up to his face, and gave it a gentle kiss. Kirsten's face flushed even more as Gabriel's eyes never broke contact with hers as he kissed her hand. Kirsten softly inhaled and could catch the hint of his cologne. Cinnamon and cedarwood were the dominant smells. Gabriel had worn the same fragrance when they first met, and it was magic for Kirsten, who felt her mind melt a little when she smelled it. Allison quietly excused herself from the couple. As she did, Gabriel turned to acknowledge Allison's departure with a subtle, gentle nod.

"You look amazing," Gabriel finally said, looking back at Kirsten.

"Thanks... uh... you, too," Kirsten responded meekly, struggling to make the words come out.

"Do you want a drink?" Gabriel asked, shifting his body, gesturing to the bar behind him.

"Yes," Kirsten said as she put her left hand in Gabriel's open right. Grabbing her hand, Gabriel led the way as they walked to the bar.

"I feel like I'm underdressed and don't belong here," Kirsten whispered as they approached the bar.

"Really? Why?" Gabriel asked.

"Well, I look at everyone else and think, 'wow'. Then I look at me, and think, 'meh'," Kirsten explained.

"Oh?" Gabriel said as he glanced around. "I didn't notice everyone else," he continued as his gaze returned to Kirsten. "I only noticed you." Kirsten's face flushed again, and she sheepishly looked down. *Could he be any more courteous?* she thought. Gabriel's hand caught her chin and gently pulled her face up to meet his. His dark eyes felt piercing as she met them with her own. Without even thinking, she brought her face up to meet his, and they locked in a gentle kiss...

*BANG, BANG, BANG!*

The sounds broke Kirsten's thoughts suddenly with a firm knock on her door. Not realizing how much time had passed, she got up quickly and reached the door as another round of knocks came through. "Yes, yes. Hang on," Kirsten said, somewhat annoyed as she glanced through the peephole in her door.

It was Mr Fox. As she unlocked the door and opened it, Mr Fox greeted her with a soft smile and gentle nod of his head. "And here I thought you'd just appear in my home like Batman," Kirsten said teasingly.

Mr Fox chuckled. "No," he said. "I thought I'd be more 'normal' for this visit," he finished stating, making the air quotations with his fingers when he said the word normal.

Rolling her eyes with sarcasm, Kirsten smiled and opened the door wider to let him in. "Do you want anything?" Kirsten asked as Mr Fox sat down on her couch.

"No." he replied. "I'm okay. Thank you."

Mr Fox pulled a laptop out of his bag and began to bring up various windows on the screen. Kirsten sat down next to him and finally asked, "So, is it good news or not?"

Mr Fox glanced at her and then back at his laptop, saying nothing. After a few moments, he sat back and started to explain. "Your work scouting that warehouse was successful. And we've been able to identify the few people involved that we were not initially aware of and the companies attached to them. This new information, combined with the rest of the information we already had, has helped us narrow down the smugglers and their shipment schedule."

"And?" Kirsten said, unable to hide her impatient feelings.

"I also have some info in regards to your personal life," Mr Fox replied.

If Kirsten wasn't already tense and impatient, she felt it now. She took a few deep breaths to try and relax as she listened intently to what Mr Fox was about to say.

Mr Fox leaned back on the couch. "You were right."

# Chapter 10

# Revealed

"Right? What did he mean, right? Right about what?" These questions and more flashed through Kirsten's mind. Mr Fox must've seen some outward expression from Kirsten because he began explaining before Kirsten could make out the questions to ask him.

"At the warehouse," Mr Fox said plainly. Kirsten's nerves calmed somewhat.

"Which part?" Kirsten asked.

"We identified Gabriel going into the warehouse that night with the others," Mr Fox continued. "We had trouble identifying the female since her hair covered too much of her face in your photos. But because of this, I've taken the liberty of increasing surveillance on Gabriel. As well as the others that were at the warehouse that night."

Kirsten sat quiet for a moment. She wasn't sure herself but had strongly suspected the one that walked in last was Gabriel. But since it wasn't a sure thing, she let it go, and almost forgot about it entirely. "What does that mean for me now?" Kirsten inquired, her nerves starting to tense up again. Between this information and what Allison shared with her, Kirsten began to really struggle within herself about her love for him.

"Nothing changes," Mr Fox replied. "We will do more investigating on our end. Just continue on as you like."

"But how can I if what Allison said is true?"

Mr Fox let out a long hard breath before responding. "I don't have concrete information about what Allison said," he began.

Kirsten's heart sank a bit as Mr Fox went on to explain that any coverage of Gabriel they had only involved the times when she was with him or if he crossed paths with the others they were already watching or members of his office. Mr Fox did reassure Kirsten, though, that since he's been positively identified with the group as one of them, his activities are now closely monitored. Mr Fox showed Kirsten a number of camera shots on his laptop that revealed parts of Gabriel's condo, office, and parking garage.

"I've been dating Gabriel almost a year, and you are only now watching him closely?" Kirsten snapped, now more frustrated than relieved.

"Had no reason to," Mr Fox said. "We were gathering intel on the others we knew about, and Gabriel didn't show up on our radar until recently. We didn't think it necessary to disrupt your relationship beyond a basic background check, which he passed."

"Still," Kirsten retorted as she crossed her arms in disgust and leaned back in her chair.

"If anything comes up, you will be the first to be notified," Mr Fox said, closing his laptop. "We are so close," he finished.

"I hope so," Kirsten said, breathing out a sigh of relief and calmed down now that she processed what just took place.

"I'll leave you to it then," Mr Fox said as he stood to leave. Kirsten didn't move apart from a head nod to acknowledge Mr Fox's departure. Once he left, Kirsten sat alone and quiet for several minutes, replaying what just happened. Even if Gabriel wasn't cheating, his involvement in the investigation of Mr Fox still put her on edge.

Kirsten got ready for bed and tried to sleep. Her brain,

however, had different plans. It would seem as Kirsten tried to get comfortable, her thoughts wandered back again to Gabriel and her time with him...

Kirsten looked up into Gabriel's eyes. Her head was resting in his lap. They had been watching a movie together having a quiet night in. Gabriel glanced down at her and smiled softly. "What?" he asked playfully.

"Nothing," Kirsten responded in kind. "Just looking."

Gabriel's smile strengthened as he looked back up at the TV and moved his hand up to rest it on Kirsten's chest just below her neck. Kirsten brought her hand up to touch it as she turned her head back to the movie. It had been a couple of months now, and Kirsten still felt like she did when they first met.

Kirsten and Gabriel had been keeping it somewhat casual as far the relationship title went. However, as time went on, neither one could deny the strength of the feelings between each other. They only usually got together on weekends, and they hadn't talked about moving in together. Still, when they were together, it was nothing but emotional fire between them; and tonight, was no different.

After a few more minutes, Kirsten got up. Gabriel looked slightly puzzled as he asked what was up — expecting Kirsten to either grab food, a drink, or go to the bathroom. Gabriel was pleasantly surprised when Kirsten grabbed his hand. His face met hers as Kirsten leaned in and planted a soft kiss on Gabriel's cheek. As Kirsten stood back up, still smiling, she gave Gabriel's hand a gentle tug. Gabriel smiled as he knew instantly what was being asked of him and got up off the couch himself.

Kirsten led Gabriel to her bedroom, and he shut the door behind them. Gabriel pressed Kirsten against the wall, holding her hands up above her head. Gabriel pressed in closer, teasing

Kirsten by bringing his face close to hers, only to pull away just out of reach for her to kiss him. After a moment, Kirsten relaxed. The scent of Gabriel's cedarwood and cinnamon cologne again made Kirsten weak.

Gabriel let go of Kirsten's hands but stood still, keeping his body close. Kirsten ran her hands up his chest, pulling Gabriel's shirt with them. The two locked lips as Gabriel's shirt cleared his face; he picked up Kirsten and carried her to bed...

*BEEP! BEEP! BEEP!*

Kirsten awoke to her alarm going off, and after a moment, reluctantly forced herself up and turned it off. She wasn't sure when she fell asleep, but it must've been later than expected because she felt exhausted. After sitting in bed for a few moments, Kirsten finally got up and got ready for work.

Work was hard for Kirsten today as thoughts of Gabriel and Allison flashed through her mind repeatedly. She had texted Gabriel right before lunch, hoping that being with him would help her. Allison hadn't texted or called yet. Though it was no surprise to Kirsten, Allison would give it a day or so, and then reach out as she usually had, the few times they had disagreements.

Kirsten was finishing up at the gym after work when she got a text; the beep went off in her headphones, and she excitedly put down her weights and checked her phone. A feeling of disappointment came over Kirsten as she realized it was only Mr Fox.

*'We found something.' — Mr Fox*
*'Meet at your place, ASAP.' — Mr Fox*

Kirsten wasted no time and rushed home. She hated how vague Mr Fox was when it came to this lately. Because now, as she drove home, Kirsten had a dozen different things racing through her mind about what it could be.

When Kirsten got home, she opened her apartment to find Mr Fox already sitting in her living room with his laptop open on the coffee table. Before she could say anything, Mr Fox motioned to her to come quickly and sit next to him. Kirsten promptly dropped her bag and sat on the couch next to Mr Fox. He handed her a headset to listen and put a pair on his head as well.

"We don't have visuals because they are in his car, and we only have an audio bug in there," Mr Fox explained while he brought up the feed.

"Whose car?" asked Kirsten quickly.

"Gabriel's," Mr Fox said. "Allison is with him."

"How long have they been there?"

"Not long," Mr Fox answered. "We heard them arrange the meeting, and that's when I called you. They met in Gabriel's office parking lot right before you showed up."

"But wha..." Kirsten started to say, but she was cut off as the voices started coming through her headset as Mr Fox tuned into that frequency.

"I don't know," Allison said. Whatever she acknowledged was missed before Mr Fox got his equipment connected.

"I'm serious," Gabriel said. "That panty liner you left in my trash caused some major un-needed stress."

"But you explained it away," Allison responded. "And it really just helped plant the seeds to have her leave."

"Yea, except we still need her, and I'm hoping to flip her," Gabriel started to say. "This has to stop. I don't need the extra drama in my life and I want to keep her."

"But I've already set the stage for this," Allison said softly. "And I'll keep directing her that way if I need to. I think she's outlasted her usefulness."

Gabriel exhaled heavily. "I don't want her hurt, and the operation is starting to get more heat from the authorities, and I don't want her caught up in that."

"You can always break up with her," Allison said.

"No," Gabriel snapped. "I can't. I don't want to, and I just said we still need her yet."

"Get rid of her," Allison said firmly. Her toned changed and she sounded more authoritative. "Or I will create a bunch of problems you don't need."

"Is that a threat?" Gabriel asked calmly. "You are aware of what I do, right? And you are replaceable."

"I'm well aware," Allison stated. "But you have more to lose than I do right now. And you are just as replaceable as I am."

Some shuffling noises were heard, and then Mr Fox and Kirsten heard a door shut. Allison must have left because only a minute later, the music in Gabriel's car started to play, and the engine revved up. Any chance of hearing any other conversations was now useless.

Kirsten just sat quiet and removed her headset. "Act natural around Gabriel until we know more," Mr Fox began. "This isn't going to be easy, and I can't tell you how to respond. But I will advise that we go with it for now."

Kirsten nodded quickly. Tears had already formed in her eyes as she knew what was coming. She wasn't ready for it. Honestly, Kirsten had hoped her relationship could continue and not be involved in this mess. Mr Fox closed up his computer and put the rest of his equipment in his bag. He glanced at Kirsten. She didn't move or acknowledge him. After a brief moment, Mr Fox got up and put his hand on Kirsten's shoulder.

Kirsten felt his hand and quickly snapped out of her thoughts. Kirsten began to wipe the tears away from her eyes, and with that, Mr Fox left. Once he was gone, Kirsten jumped in the shower and sat down under the water. She started to cry again as more memories flashed through her mind...

Kirsten woke up with the sun shining on her face. As she got up and cleared her eyes, the room became brighter. Kirsten realized that the curtains on the bedroom patio doors were open, and the morning sunlight filled the room. *"Gabriel's room was so perfect,"* Kirsten thought. She loved the way the morning sun came in and reflected off the walls. Kirsten rolled over in bed, stretching as she did. The smooth sheets felt great against her skin.

Glancing across the bed, Kirsten noticed that Gabriel was gone. *"That's strange,"* Kirsten thought as she sat up. Her head was aching again, but it seemed to be fading as she got up, so she dismissed it. The bathroom door was still open, and she didn't see him in there, so Kirsten grabbed Gabriel's shirt from the floor to put on.

Kirsten was still buttoning the shirt as she got out into the main part of the condo. Suddenly the scent of breakfast foods hit her nose. Kirsten inhaled deeply as she walked towards the source. Kirsten stepped into the kitchen and just smiled as Gabriel was busy cooking.

Gabriel noticed Kirsten almost immediately and turned to greet her.

"Hey, sleepyhead," Gabriel said as he smiled. Gabriel was wearing just some grey lounging pants and nothing else.

"Good morning," Kirsten said as she playfully walked towards him, exaggerating her movements to tease him.

Gabriel grabbed Kirsten's waist as she got close enough to pull in. Holding her tight, Gabriel brought his head down and gave her a tight but comfortable hug. Kirsten could still smell hints of his cologne from the night prior, and the strength of his arms made her melt. Suddenly, before she knew what was happening, Gabriel had picked her up and set her on the counter. Sitting there, Kirsten opened her legs and let Gabriel get closer. His hands on her waist, and Kirsten's hands still locked gently behind his neck.

"I'm so lucky to have met you." Gabriel finally said.

Kirsten smiled softly and almost blushed. "I'm also very lucky to have you. I…" Kirsten's words were cut off as Gabriel came up and kissed her as she spoke. So many feelings, so many emotions…

The memory faded out as Kirsten sat in her shower. The water had moved from hot to room temperature, but Kirsten didn't care. She continued to sit there with the water running over her for some time yet. The tears had stopped, but the feelings remained; so many pieces, so many things to consider.

Kirsten couldn't believe that it was Allison who was trying to break them up. So then the 'other woman' must've been made up. And Gabriel defended Kirsten and their relationship with Allison in a way, which made Kirsten feel a little better about how Gabriel felt. However, the fact remained that he and Allison were up to something together. And what about the operation that Gabriel mentioned. So many things raced through Kirsten's mind as she finally crawled out of the now cold shower.

Kirsten checked her phone before going to bed. No notifications. As she lay there still emotionally torn, Kirsten texted her boss that she would be taking tomorrow off sick. Kirsten needed time to think about how to approach the situation with her friends, and being at work, at least for now, wasn't going to help.

## Chapter 11

## Discovery

The next day, Kirsten lay in bed for most of the morning. She was switching between lying there lost in thoughts and browsing her phone. The night was rough for Kirsten, and she was in no hurry to move about her day. Allison and Gabriel hadn't texted or called yet. Not that Kirsten was expecting them to, but if they didn't know that she knew what happened last night, then they should still treat her like the ignorant friend she had been.

It was around lunch when Kirsten finally got up and dressed for the day. As she sat down in her living room eating, she decided she should text Gabriel. To fully understand what was going on, she needed to get him to talk more. Additionally, to not come off as suspicious to him or Allison, Kirsten thought it best to act naturally and not directly ask or address the recent developments and see how they responded.

*'Hey, babe. Did you want to get together tonight?'* — Kirsten
*'Not able to tonight. I have a late meeting. But tomorrow for sure!'* — Gabriel

Kirsten was shocked that she got an immediate response. Thoughts and feelings came up as she read the text. Kirsten didn't know what to think. On the one hand, her love for Gabriel was still there. She felt happy that he still wanted to see her. On the other hand, she was sad again because of what she overheard Gabriel and Allison talking about last night.

*'No worries, tomorrow will be fine. I love you.'* — *Kirsten*
*'I love you too!'* — *Gabriel*

Kirsten's heart sank, both from happiness and sadness, as she grappled with the idea of that message. Memories and feelings rushed through Kirsten as she sat there in the silence of her apartment…

The wind blew Kirsten's hair as she sped along the highway. She and Gabriel had just finished a good dinner and were heading back to her place for the night. The weather was hot and sunny, so Gabriel had the convertible top down as they drove. Kirsten was holding Gabriel's hand, each of them exchanging loving glances at each other as they went.

The sun was almost set by the time they got to Kirsten's place. After getting inside, the two got comfortable on the couch and started watching a movie. Gabriel sat on the end of the sofa with Kirsten snuggled up to his right side, holding his hand as she did so.

As the movie played, the two enjoyed some laughs and a little small talk. After some time, Kirsten picked her head up off Gabriel's shoulder that she had been using to rest it on. Gabriel turned to look at Kirsten whose eyes were already fixed on him. Gabriel smiled softly as he gazed deep into her eyes. Gabriel knew what he felt; he knew what he wanted.

Kirsten, leaving her left hand still holding Gabriel's right and resting in his lap, reached up with her right and touched Gabriel's cheek. Gabriel closed his eyes and rested his head into her hand. Kirsten then brought her face up to kiss him, a soft kiss that felt more emotional than physical. Kirsten dropped her hand to Gabriel's chest, and after a moment, she looked up and finally said, "I need to tell you something."

"Say it," Gabriel said softly, yet intensely. "I know what you want to say." Kirsten blushed a bit and glanced down for a moment before composing herself and attempting to speak. As she glanced back up at Gabriel's face, Kirsten felt the emotions rise. She tried to talk, but after failing to do so, she rested her head against his. Forehead to forehead, Gabriel shifted his body to face Kirsten more directly, keeping his contact with her.

"Maybe this will help you," Gabriel said as he pulled his head away from Kirsten's to look directly into her eyes. "I love you," Gabriel finally said after a moment of silence.

Kirsten's heart was pounding hard as she heard the words. They had been together now for about six months, and though this was the first time the words were finally spoken, it had been a long time coming.

"I love you, too," Kirsten said as tears of emotion formed in her eyes. She went in to kiss Gabriel again. The two locked together, and Kirsten put her hands upon Gabriel's face and laid back, pulling him on top of her. The connection was more intense now. Every touch, every kiss, the feelings were stronger than they had been before...

Kirsten was still looking at her phone. The screen had timed out and was just blank, and Kirsten, after snapping out of her mind and the memory. Hit the button again to open up the phone. The text message screen was still up, and Kirsten saw the message again and immediately started to fall back into her thoughts and sadness.

*BEEP! BEEP!*

Kirsten was shaken out of her regression, this time by her phone's text notification. Checking the phone, she saw that it was Mr Fox. Kirsten hesitated before opening the text. She couldn't possibly take more bad news now.

*'Meet me at Ocean Sands Hotel. Room 334. Six p.m.'* — *Mr Fox*

*'Okay.'* — *Kirsten*

Kirsten cleaned her apartment a bit and then just sat and watched a movie. Trying to keep her mind off things proved more difficult than she hoped. Allison still hadn't reached out, but Kirsten wasn't worried, nor did she care at this point. Having both her best friend and boyfriend turn against her together and at the same time was more than Kirsten was ready to handle.

At six p.m. on the nose, Kirsten knocked on the hotel door as instructed. Mr Fox answered promptly and let her in.

"I'm glad you're here," Mr Fox said, inviting her further into the room. Kirsten walked in and noticed that Mr Fox was not alone. A whole surveillance team was poised inside the room with all kinds of equipment.

"Who are all these people?" Kirsten asked as she glanced around, processing the surroundings.

"My team. And that's all you need to know," Mr Fox replied. "Follow me," he continued as he motioned for Kirsten to follow. The men paid little attention to her as she passed their workstations. They walked into the adjoining room where the lights were off and the curtains were mostly drawn. As they approached the window, Mr Fox motioned for Kirsten to look through the spotting scope set up in the window and posed just out the main view to not be easily spotted by those on the outside.

Kirsten looked through the scope and noticed it was Gabriel's office. Gabriel and Allison were there along with several other men. She recognized most of them as the men she met at the fundraiser where she met Gabriel for the first time.

Of the ones she recognized, some of them were the same

men she saw at the warehouse that night she was doing recon. They were all sitting around a conference table. Kirsten felt a nudge and glanced up to see Mr Fox holding some headphones. Kirsten put them on, and Mr Fox had donned a set for himself. Kirsten noticed that Mr Fox was using a laptop and was looking at the same view as the scope that Kirsten was looking through.

Kirsten looked back through the scope, and suddenly the voices came in through her headset loud and clear as if she was in the room herself.

"Are we ready?" Gabriel asked the group as he stood up from the table. Murmurs of agreement came out from the others at the table. "Good," Gabriel said. "The last shipments are on time, and we have the warehouse ready to receive the freight."

"Are the port authorities going to interrupt us?" said one of the other men at the table.

"No, I've taken care of that. We will have free reign as we have for all of our shipments," said another.

"Perfect," Gabriel said.

"What of Kirsten?" Allison asked almost cynically.

Gabriel just tightened his jaw and glared back. "No," he stated firmly. The other men around the table appeared to be divided over his answer.

One man spoke out and said, "Gabriel, you did a good job of keeping her away from the warehouse after you got back from Vegas. But her car was still seen nearby that following week, when we met."

Before Gabriel could respond, another piped in. "I'm not concerned about Kirsten, but I am concerned about whom she may be working with." Then he turned to Allison and continued, "I know that she was needed initially, and your informant was extremely helpful in allowing us to select her, but I agree with you now that her usefulness is overshadowed by her liability."

Kirsten froze in terror for a moment before glancing at Mr Fox, who was already looking shocked as he looked at Kirsten. Cautiously now, Kirsten looked back through the scope and kept listening.

Allison was smiling smugly at Gabriel in response to the comments just made. More men jumped in and argued back and forth. Kirsten couldn't make out all the words as some were louder than others, and each was talking over the other. Overall, the men were relatively calm in their body language during this part of the discussion, despite the difference of opinions. Allison continued sitting there, a cocky smile still on her face watching it all unfold. Gabriel just stood there at the head of the table and waited for a moment to cut in.

"Enough," Gabriel finally snapped after several minutes. The room quieted. Each member adjusted to get comfortable in their seats again and looked at Gabriel. "If — and in mean if — Kirsten becomes a problem, I will take care of it," Gabriel said. His tone was firm, clear, and authoritative.

"What's the plan then?" one of the men asked.

"The plan? The plan is to see if she can be a part of this eventually," Gabriel answered. "I have waited long enough. I think she could be helpful to me in this long term."

The men glanced at each other and back at Allison, then back up to Gabriel. "We will let it ride for now," said the man who first spoke. "You've been a valuable asset, and we trust your judgment. We understand that we need her. But not at the risk of our operation."

Gabriel nodded in acceptance.

"But make no mistake," the man said again. "If this goes south, and she's involved, we *will* deal with it, and you." Then, as he stood, he asked Gabriel, "Are we meeting at the warehouse later tonight?"

Gabriel nodded again. And with that, the men started to leave. Gabriel sat back down in his chair as the men funneled out. Allison sat across the table as she had been, unmoved. After the men left, Allison got up and slowly walked towards Gabriel.

"Are you sure you want to keep her?" Allison asked as she moved closer.

Gabriel held up his pointer finger, gesturing to Allison to wait or stay back. Allison didn't listen and kept walking towards him. Putting her hands on Gabriel's shoulders, she gave them a tight squeeze as if she was massaging them. Gabriel's head dropped into his hand that was propped up on the arm of the chair.

"Don't Allison, please," Gabriel said softly.

"Don't?" Allison repeated. "Why? We did it before, and Kirsten doesn't have to know."

"You blackmailed me with information that I couldn't reveal yet. And I will know, and that's enough for me," Gabriel said firmly.

"Was it that bad?" Allison said as she leaned forward, bending over Gabriel's shoulder, moved her hands down his chest to his stomach, and started unbuttoning his shirt.

Gabriel grabbed her hands and stopped them from going further. Moving his head out from under Allison's arms, Gabriel stood up and turned to face her. Allison made a smug smile and then jumped in and gave Gabriel a peck on the lips. Gabriel jerked back but was too slow. Allison planted the kiss anyway.

"No. I love Kirsten, and I will stay with her," Gabriel said.

"You better change that to a yes. Or I'll tell Kirsten everything," said Allison.

Without warning, Allison was suddenly thrown down

against the table. Before she could protest, Gabriel had her face pinned against the table by pressing the back of her throat. Allison used her hands to push back off the table. But Gabriel was too strong and held her down. She was afraid at first but then felt Gabriel lift up her skirt and heard him undo his belt. He was so rough and hard, almost hurting her, but Allison didn't say anything, just moans of acceptance.

Kirsten watched and listened. When she saw what was happening, she turned away at first, unable to watch it unfold. After a moment, she glanced back into the scope and saw Gabriel's face. Tears were running down his cheeks as he continued, his face was tense and he looked angry. Allison's face winced in pain against the tabletop. Kirsten then pulled away, feeling sick to her stomach. She saw enough as she ripped off her headset and ran to the closest trashcan to vomit.

Mr Fox pulled off his headset and motioned one of the techs there to grab a towel and some water. As Kirsten finished throwing up, she leaned back and sat on the floor against the wall. Tears were streaking down her face now. Mr Fox crouched down next to her and handed her the towel. Kirsten accepted it and wiped her face. "I'm so sorry," Mr Fox finally said. "Had I known, I would've just told you after the fact and spared you the details and the visual."

Kirsten nodded in understanding. "I know. Thank you," she said after drinking some of the water that was brought to her.

Mr Fox motioned to the same guy that grabbed the towel to come back. Mr Fox pulled the man down to sit next to them on the floor and proceeded to talk in hushed tones. "Find the mole, and find the connection to Allison," Mr Fox said. "We need to know how long they've been fed information and what has been exposed." The man nodded and got up to leave, but Mr Fox held him down for a moment more. "Trust no one with this," he finished. The man nodded again and got up to return to his station.

Kirsten was getting up at the same time and Mr Fox turned to her, "Where are you going?" he asked.

"Home."

And with that, Kirsten left the hotel room. Mr Fox stood there for a moment after she left, then turned to one of the other techs and said, "Track her. She's not going home. I won't have her blow this operation over a heartache. And get someone down to the warehouse."

Kirsten got in her car and sat a moment before starting it. Her sadness turned to boiling anger. Anger at both Gabriel and Allison, though Allison was for sure the main point of her rage. Having them lie to her about when he got back from Vegas. Gabriel must've been who Allison got the call from.

Then she remembered what she heard Allison say on the phone that night in the club parking lot. *"... 'That's ridiculous,' Allison snapped after a few seconds of silence. 'Of course, she doesn't know.'... 'Yea, I'll let her know and meet you there.'"* Kirsten didn't have enough pieces to have an accurate picture. However, based on what she overheard then and now, Gabriel was likely the call that Allison took that night, and they had met up after Kirsten was dropped off at home.

The images of Gabriel and Allison tonight flashed again in Kirsten's mind. She hit her steering wheel a few times and screamed under her breath. How could Allison do this to her? How long was it going on? How many times did it happen? What was the driving factor? Kirsten needed to know the answers. And with that, Kirsten decided to head to Allison's condo. She would confront her in person.

Kirsten couldn't speak to Gabriel yet. She still loved him but struggled with how to approach it. Possibly after clearing things up with Allison, she could sit down with Gabriel and get his side. Tears started forming as she drove, a mix of anger and sadness. Allison was going to pay for this.

# Chapter 12

# Confrontation

Kirsten arrived at Allison's place later that evening. Kirsten knew the gate code and proceeded into the parking area of the complex. She didn't see Allison's car in her parking spot, so she was sure Allison hadn't returned yet. Kirsten parked some distance away to keep Allison from seeing her car when she got there. Cautiously, Kirsten picked the lock on Allison's apartment door; it was silent enough, but she didn't want an unsuspecting resident to see her. Once she was inside, Kirsten headed to the security alarm and punched in the code. Allison had mentioned to Kirsten some time ago that she made it the same as the gate code so she could easily remember it.

Kirsten, still teeming with anger and hurt, decided to search her place since Allison was gone and see if she could find anything. After searching for a while, trying to be careful about what she touched and where she looked, still, Kirsten found nothing; afterward, she sat down in a chair in Allison's living room. And there, Kirsten waited; she didn't know when or if Allison would be back there, or go straight to the warehouse. She decided to wait a bit before finally leaving and going home.

*BEEP! BEEP!*

Two quick beeps from Kirsten's phone meant a text message had just come through. Kirsten pulled out her phone and saw that Mr Fox had sent her something.

*'Please don't do anything stupid.'* — Mr Fox

*'I'm just going to talk to Allison about her telling me to break up with Gabriel and see what she says.'* — Kirsten

*'I won't mention tonight or anything about what we know.'* — Kirsten

*'Good.'* — Mr Fox

*'Because she is on her way to you now.'* — Mr Fox

*'???'* — Kirsten

*'Don't play dumb. She is heading to her house now, I know you are there. ETA ten min.'* — Mr Fox

Kirsten's heart quickened. She had calmed down a bit during the time that she was searching Allison's house. Now, however, with the knowledge that Allison was on her way and very close. Kirsten began to run through what would happen and the hypothetical responses to the impending conversation. It didn't take long for Kirsten to get re-worked up about what happened.

Moments later, Kirsten heard Allison coming in the door. Kirsten had already turned out the lights and was standing quietly off to the side. Kirsten decided to play coy at first and catch Allison off guard. This would hopefully allow Kirsten to see how Allison played her cards. Kirsten's heart was in her throat, and her stomach was tight. Brief images of what she saw in that conference room just moments earlier flashed in Kirsten's mind. She couldn't shake them. Seeing Gabriel and Allison like that was frozen in her brain.

As Allison stepped further into the front room and turned on the light, she noticed that her alarm was turned off and glanced around cautiously. Allison's place was bigger than Kirsten's with more space and bigger rooms. Allison stepped down the hall to her left and into her bedroom and glancing around to see who was there. When she didn't see anyone, she cautiously approached her bathroom. When that looked clear, she continued back to the main living area.

"I haven't heard from you in a while," Kirsten said casually as she stepped out from the doorway to the kitchen towards the back of the room. She folded her arms across her chest and stood strong, and glared questioningly at Allison. Allison let out a soft scream and jumped a little as Kirsten did so.

"Holy sh..." Allison started and breathed heavily as words trailed off. "What are you doing in my house?" she finished.

"Whatcha been up to?" Kirsten asked firmly, stepping forward and dropping her arms.

"Work and such, you know...?" Allison's words trailed off as she thought. She then realized that Gabriel must've said something since Kirsten was here. Allison became furious as she thought this. The possibility that Gabriel went crying to Kirsten to confess everything made her frustration flare up. Allison stepped forward towards Kirsten in a defensive response and continued, "He told you, didn't he?"

Kirsten didn't say anything. She couldn't, even if she wanted to, she was still processing everything and didn't want to say something that would hint at what she knew. "Of course he did," Allison continued, after acknowledging the pause. "He has a soft spot for you, and it's becoming increasingly more annoying."

Kirsten stepped forward; she was within an arm's reach of Allison now. All her muscles were tense. "How could you do this to me?" she exclaimed, trying to hide some of her emotions and failing slightly. *Just play along to get more information,* she thought.

"Shut up," Allison snapped.

Before Kirsten knew what happened, Allison had punched her so quickly she didn't even have a chance to block it. Allison had connected square with Kirsten's nose sending her stumbling back and grabbing her nose. Allison stood still, Kirsten, now standing up straight, facing her. Blood running down her face, Kirsten wiped it with her hand and posed, ready to fight.

Allison wasn't concerned, she knew she could beat Kirsten. Allison had been fight-training for a long time because of her role in her job with Gabriel and the others. She never let on about how much she knew, however, because Allison loved to see the shock on people's faces when she would have to fight them. The shock usually created a moment of hesitation of surprise in her opponents that she could usually use to her advantage.

"You have interfered with this long enough," Allison said, charging forward to attack Kirsten.

"Interfered with what?" Kirsten exclaimed, as she blocked the incoming blows.

"You know what," Allison said as she charged forward and kept swinging.

Kirsten was surprised at how well Allison fought. She knew about her own skill and training, but she did not expect Allison to be such an even match. Kirsten ducked and dodged the first couple of blows but then started to return with her own. Allison did her best, but Kirsten was quick and managed to front kick Allison back. Kirsten used this moment to re-center herself and face Allison if she came at her again. She wanted to fight Allison, more than anything, but Kirsten knew that she also needed Allison to talk. So she waited to see if Allison had had enough yet.

Allison grabbed her stomach as she stumbled backwards, realizing in that moment that Kirsten also had some training. Keeping her eyes fixed on Kirsten, Allison caught her breath and smiled. Allison was almost happy that Kirsten would be a decent fight; it had been a while and Allison's frustration with the situation, and with Kirsten, made this perfect.

Before continuing, while still watching Kirsten's position, Allison reached down as she brought her foot up to her hand and took off her heels one at time. After tossing them to the side, Allison reached under skirt, and started to remove her thong. Kirsten made a brief puzzled look wondering what Allison could be thinking. Until she saw that Allison took her thong, wrapped it in her fingers and then used it to quickly tie her hair back into a pony tail.

Allison, almost sensually, licked her fingers afterward as if she was cleaning them off. She didn't know for sure that Kirsten knew what had just happened with Gabriel, she suspected Gabriel had told Kirsten something since she was here in Allison's apartment confronting her. Nevertheless, Allison licked her fingers and smiled as she did.

Kirsten watched and stayed ready, when Allison licked her fingers and smiled, at first Kirsten didn't get it, until after Allison had finished. Then Kirsten realized what Allison was rubbing in her face by doing that. Upon this realization, Kirsten lost her shit, and charged Allison.

Exchanging blow for blow, the ladies fought, moving throughout the house. Both ladies' clothes were being torn, and Allison's stuff was being broken all over. Kirsten managed to grab a magazine and roll it up tight to use it against Allison. It worked for a bit as she managed to catch Allison in the face a couple of times before Allison finally grabbed that arm, and through a judo roll, managed to throw Kirsten to the ground and disarm her of the makeshift weapon.

Allison continued to kick and hit Kirsten while holding her arm and keeping her on the floor. Kirsten then found her opening and kicked Allison's left knee hard enough to make Allison flinch and allow Kirsten a moment to regain her feet. As Kirsten got up, she front-kicked Allison square in the solar plexus, much harder this second time, and sent Allison flying backward into the wall. Kirsten stood still a moment and massaged her shoulder, rotating her arm to help ease the pain of the brace that Allison had just had her in.

Kirsten wouldn't have long, however, as Allison quickly regained her breath and charged forward again. Kirsten was ready this time and immediately deflected Allison's first punch and grabbed that wrist, and twisted it, forcing Allison to pause before swinging her left arm to try and break free. Kirsten blocked Allison's attempts at striking with her free hand and only tightened the hold on Allison's right. Allison grunted with pain but then jumped up, flipping over, which twisted her wrist back to the proper place, and proceeded to punch through Kirsten's grip, breaking free.

The two continued fighting, pressing each other using anything they could grab to use as a weapon. Finally, Kirsten got behind Allison and held her in a tight chokehold.

"I don't want to ever see you again," Kirsten muttered in Allison's ear, still holding tight.

Allison gasped for air, grabbing at Kirsten's arm, which was still wrapped around her throat, slowly squeezing tighter. "Don't worry. You won't," Allison finally said. And with that, she kicked up with her left leg, coming straight up and connected with Kirsten's head over her right shoulder. Kirsten let go just enough that Allison was then able to pull free. Kirsten was still a little out of it as Allison spun around to face her and quickly grabbed Kirsten's head and brought her knee up, connecting hard and knocking Kirsten out cold.

Allison breathed heavily as she regained her composure, staring at Kirsten's seemingly lifeless body lying on the floor near her. Allison glanced around her place, holes in the drywall, blood spatters in various areas, and a general look of dishevelment as she relived what just happened. Allison ripped the power cords out of her TV and DVD player and used them to tie Kirsten's hands and feet. She didn't want Kirsten waking up and attacking again.

Afterward, Allison carefully walked to the bathroom, limping more than walking as the adrenaline wore off and the pain in her knee started to come through from when Kirsten kicked it. Once in the bathroom, Allison noticed that her clothes were completely torn apart. She had lost her jacket in the fight, but her blouse was barely held together as well as her bra underneath.

Rips and bloodstains all over, her makeshift ponytail had all but completely fallen out and her makeup was a mess. Allison took off her skirt and blouse and just threw them into the trash, washed up, and quickly changed. She needed to get to Gabriel, talk to him about what happened, and find out what he told Kirsten.

It only took Allison a few minutes to put herself together and she walked back out into the main area. Kirsten was still out, so Allison untied her and left. She wasn't worried about what Kirsten may or may not have known at this point. And it's doubtful she would go to the police for this fight, and there was nothing in her apartment that Kirsten would find or be interested in.

But she didn't need the police to find Kirsten tied up in her place. So, at the moment, it seemed better to Allison to let her go. Allison was sure that Kirsten would just wake up and leave, she'd probably try to contact Gabriel, but by that time Allison will have already gotten to him. Allison got in her car and headed to the warehouse on the docks. She and Gabriel, needed to talk…

… Kirsten came to with a soft groan. Picking herself up carefully, feeling around to check for any significant damage. She wasn't sure how long she'd been out for. As she regained more of her senses, the pain from the fight started to come. Her shoulder was on fire, and her head was throbbing. She found some blood, but it was almost dry, so Kirsten wasn't too concerned with that.

The room was dark. It took a moment for Kirsten to remember where she was. But as quickly as the pain came, the memories did, too. Kirsten got up slowly wondering where Allison had gone and if she was waiting for her. She walked to the bathroom and turned on the light. Kirsten's clothes were torn a bit, and blood was everywhere. Although, a closer examination revealed that nothing was still profusely bleeding. Even her nose had stopped bleeding at this point.

Kirsten then noticed Allison's clothes in the trash and realized that she must be gone. Not wanting to draw attention, Kirsten cleaned up as best she could. Thankfully, her clothes weren't terrible, but she grabbed one of Allison's sweaters to wear over her clothes to keep from drawing too much attention as she exited the complex. Kirsten washed her face, fixed her hair and let it fall in front to hide her face, and left the condo.

Kirsten texted Gabriel right away as she got to her car asking when they could get together tomorrow. She was hoping that he would still agree to meet even though Allison had most likely already gotten to him and told him what happened. Gabriel didn't respond right away, but that was okay for now. Kirsten needed to get home and clean up.

*BEEP! BEEP!*

Kirsten checked her phone as she drove. Mr Fox had sent her a text.

'How is everything?' — *Mr Fox*

'Fine, I think.' — *Kirsten*

'Allison is at the warehouse now.' — *Mr Fox*

'I'm on my way home.' — *Kirsten*

'I know, I've already got someone else on the docks.' — *Mr Fox*

'I'll hopefully try to get with Gabriel tomorrow.' — *Kirsten*

'Keep me posted.' — *Mr Fox*

Kirsten continued home in silence. When she got home her phone notification went off again. Kirsten checked it and saw that Gabriel had responded to her message.

'I can grab you in the morning for brunch.' — *Gabriel*

'Perfect!' — *Kirsten*

'Awesome. I'll call tomorrow.' — *Gabriel*

'Okay.' — *Kirsten*

Kirsten took a long shower and tried to clean up. She texted her boss again to say that she wasn't yet feeling better and would need another day off. Leading into the weekend, this would give Kirsten time to heal from her physical wounds, but also, her mental ones as well. Hopefully she would have some answers and be able to move forward.

# Chapter 13

# Allison

As Allison made her way to her car, she was simultaneously calling Gabriel. The first attempt when to voicemail, but as Allison drove, she tried calling again and got through.

"What?" Gabriel's annoyed tone could be heard through her car speakers as he answered the call.

"We have a problem," Allison said sharply.

"What now?"

"Kirsten knows," Allison started to explain. "I just left her unconscious in my condo."

"Wait. Hold up. What happened? And knows what?" Gabriel's voice grew tense as he spoke.

Allison took a few minutes to explain to Gabriel about finding Kirsten in the apartment and the confrontation that followed.

"Meet me at the warehouse," Gabriel said after a brief pause. "I'm already here going over the final details of this shipment coming in."

"Already on my way," Allison said as she hung up.

It would be a few minutes until Allison reached the warehouse. As she parked, she noticed several vehicles there. *Good,* she thought, *now I'll be able to convince them to get rid of Kirsten permanently.* Allison walked inside and approached the table where Gabriel and the others from the meeting they had earlier were standing. They were looking at a chart and a few spreadsheets. Allison couldn't make out what they were saying, but as she approached, they stopped talking and all turned to look at her.

"Well, looks like you got rung through the wringer a bit," Gabriel said. He was trying not to laugh as he noticed the limp that Allison was walking with and the cuts and bruises on her face and lip.

Allison just made a wincing face at him and stuck out her tongue sarcastically. "So what are we going to do about this?" she said as she got to the group. "I assume you've told them."

Gabriel stood up straight before speaking, "Yes. I have," he started. "And we are in agreement about what should be done."

"Good," Allison snapped, glancing around at the others. "So what are we doing then?"

Gabriel had casually glanced down at the table as Allison spoke. Once Allison finished Gabriel looked up at her. "We." He paused before continuing. "We, will not do anything. I will. And I will do it my way. You will stay out of it. You've jeopardized this operation enough by pitting her against me and causing this fuss tonight."

"But I thought that's what we wanted?" Allison asked. "I thought we agreed that she'd already served her purpose."

"What we want. And how we get what we want. Those are two different things," Gabriel said, firmly leaning over the table at Allison. "And did you just forget the conversation we had at my office?" The other men stood silent as he continued, "We are all in agreement that Kirsten was the right target, and we need to keep her close until we finish this phase of the operation. And I'm hoping she can prove useful beyond it. You're the one who picked her based on your informant." Gabriel continued pointing at Allison. "And now you want her gone?"

Allison held her hands up in defense. "I think she's a liability now. My informant should be enough. We don't need anything else she has to offer."

"Your informant is now mine," Gabriel said as he grabbed a short metal pipe that was lying nearby. He stood it up in front of him, with both hands on top, as if it was a cane he was casually resting on the floor.

Allison glared around the room as Gabriel said that. The men there did nothing and didn't speak. "Really?" Allison asked turning back to Gabriel. "After all the work I spent getting him?"

"He was just here and is going to report that nothing eventful happened here tonight to Mr Fox," one of the men finally spoke.

"Okay, but what about what Kirsten knows?" Allison questioned.

"I haven't spoken to her about anything. The only liability here now, is you," Gabriel said firmly.

Allison's face made the question before she needed to speak.

"Yes, you. Because now, thanks to you, I will have to clean up the loose ends. And hope that Mr Fox hasn't been made privy to any unwanted information," Gabriel said.

"So what do you want me to do now?" Allison asked cautiously.

"Nothing," Gabriel said as he walked around the table closer to Allison.

"Good, well, I'll take my leave then," Allison finished and turned to walk away. She got only two steps before she went dark. Her body slumped to the floor.

Gabriel had spun around swinging the pipe like a baseball bat connecting with Allison's forehead as she stepped into it. Once Allison was on the floor, Gabriel knelt down to check her pulse: nothing. Gabriel got back up, and the other men looked at him as though waiting for instruction. "We proceed as planned then?" one of the men finally asked.

"Yes," Gabriel answered.

"What of her?" another asked.

Gabriel glanced back at Allison's lifeless body before responding. "We can't have her go missing," he stated. "Put her in a car accident. Make it a good one. I don't want any suspicions."

"What of the informant outside?" the man asked. "Do we care if he knows about this?"

"He's long gone now," Gabriel replied. "I told him to take off once Allison got here when we spoke earlier."

"Got it," the man answered. He motioned to another, and they carried Allison's body out.

"What of the weapon?" asked the first man.

"I'll put it in the harbor," Gabriel responded casually.

"And what of Kirsten?" the man asked again. "We need her yet, but we can't have her get too close."

"I will talk to her. Hopefully, with news of Allison's death, things will soften up," Gabriel said.

*BEEP! BEEP!*

Gabriel glanced at his phone when the text alert came through. "Speak of the devil."

"What is it?"

"Kirsten just texted me, wanting to talk."

"When?"

"Tomorrow," Gabriel said as he started typing on his phone.

And with that, the men parted ways. Before leaving, Gabriel walked to the end of the dock near the warehouse, and after glancing around to ensure no one was watching, he dropped the pipe in the water. Then he proceeded to head home.

# Chapter 14

# Kirsten

Kirsten finished in the shower and felt a little better. After taking some pain medication, she tried to relax enough to fall asleep. Images and thoughts kept running through her mind from the last few days. She couldn't pull herself away from her feelings with Gabriel but also couldn't see how she could continue with him. Even if Allison was the instigator, this last time, Allison mentioned something about him being more willing before.

As Kirsten lay there, lost in her thoughts about what happened, she remembered that Allison had mentioned something about a boy she was seeing when they talked after the club night a while ago. This thought made Kirsten both tear up and boil in anger as she thought if what Allison said then was true.

Kirsten found it hard to focus as she tried to fall asleep. It was already well after midnight, and she would still need to be functional in the morning when Gabriel came to get her. As soon as she thought about Gabriel, her mind went back again…

Kirsten stirred in her bed, "Hey babe," Gabriel's voice came ever so softly as he spoke. "Hey," he said again, a little louder this time.

Kirsten blinked a bit and rolled over to face the direction of where Gabriel's voice came from. He was leaning over her from his side of the bed. As Kirsten's eyes cleared, she smiled softly as Gabriel's face came into view. Just seeing his face made her heart skip, and feeling even the slightest touch sent chills across her skin and butterflies in her stomach.

Gabriel and Kirsten had been together for almost a year now. Looking back to Kirsten, it seemed to fly by too quickly. She and Gabriel had been spending more time together, and they had casually joked about making the move and living together, but nothing had seriously been considered yet.

Kirsten reached up and touched Gabriel's chest, and let her fingers fall gently back down. Gabriel smiled and dropped his head as he flushed a bit. "What?" Kirsten asked softly.

"Nothing," he replied as he grabbed her hand in his and brought it up to his face.

Kirsten laid there for a second and then started to get up and sit up next to him. Gabriel leaned back, using the wall to keep himself propped up somewhat. Kirsten then readjusted so she could lie down with her head on his chest. Gabriel put his arm around her, and Kirsten brought her leg up on his as she got comfortable.

Resting her head on his bare chest, Kirsten closed her eyes briefly as she enjoyed the sound and feeling of his heartbeat. Kirsten brought her hand up and rested it on Gabriel's chest near her face. Gently, she stroked her fingers across his skin. Kirsten felt Gabriel's heartbeat quicken as she touched him. Chuckling, she glanced up at his face; he was smiling back at her. Kirsten then hugged Gabriel and moved up to kiss him. "Do you want to take a few days and chill out on my yacht?" Gabriel asked as Kirsten settled back down on his chest.

"For sure. When?" Kirsten asked.

"Next week, just for a few days," Gabriel started. "Can you

get off work?"

"Definitely," Kirsten said. "I'll put the request in today."

Gabriel hugged Kirsten tighter. "Awesome," he said. "I have a surprise for you while we are out there."

Kirsten looked up at Gabriel with a questioning glance. Gabriel merely responded with a soft smile and another hug. She knew he wouldn't tell or even hint at it. Gabriel was good at keeping the secrets to his surprises. He had surprised Kirsten several times before with various gifts or trips. But this one seemed different to Kirsten. There was a deeper genuineness to his tone and his facial expression. Kirsten was excited to find out what he meant by this surprise, but she would have to wait till next week when they were on the yacht...

Kirsten awoke later that morning to a phone call from Gabriel saying he would be there in about an hour. Kirsten sat up in her bed and immediately felt the after-effects of the fight she had. Every point of contact was sore, and it felt like every muscle was swollen. Carefully, Kirsten got out of bed, and though still extremely tired, she forced herself to stretch and try and loosen up the stiff muscles.

After several painful minutes, she finally felt like she got the throbbing pain down to a dull ache and could move with minimal discomfort. Kirsten took some more pain medication and took a shower. She kept it short, so she would have enough time to try and put herself together to minimize the visual damage to herself before Gabriel arrived.

Around ten a.m. Gabriel was knocking on the door. Kirsten answered and let him in. Once in her apartment, Gabriel went for a hug; Kirsten accepted. However, as genuine as it felt from Gabriel, she found it hard to reciprocate the action. Knowing what she knew, Kirsten would need time to accept what happened and move forward with Gabriel. She would need a way to get Gabriel to talk and explain without giving away too many details of what she knew about Allison and him.

Gabriel let go as he finished the hug and very gently kissed Kirsten's forehead. Kirsten closed her eyes and inhaled softly. As she did, Kirsten found the scent of Gabriel's cologne in her nose. It was there when she hugged him. However, now it was filling her nostrils, and as much as Kirsten initially resisted, she softened her attitude towards Gabriel as she opened up to his touch. She couldn't explain how it worked and she was sure that Gabriel wore it on purpose. It was almost as though she wanted to be mad but couldn't be once she smelled the scent.

Gabriel asked to sit down, and they turned to step further into her apartment and sat on the couch. Gabriel and Kirsten stayed close to each other, but both turned to face one another better before speaking.

Gabriel grabbed Kirsten's hands in his and bowed his head. "I'm so sorry," he said, very solemnly. Kirsten felt herself get choked up a bit but held her composure to allow Gabriel to finish. "I'm so sorry," Gabriel said again as he raised his head. "I haven't been the boyfriend you deserve. Nor have I treated you like the girlfriend I want to spend my life with."

Kirsten was quiet but feeling for him and happy to be receiving some answers and apologies. She brought her hand up to his face and touched his cheek. "I still love you," she said. Tears were forming in her eyes. "But you must let me in. Please don't keep me in the dark," she continued softly. "I want to be a part of your life, but I can't if you don't let me."

Gabriel nodded softly. Tears were forming in his own eyes as he continued, "I love you so much, and I don't want to lose you." He paused for a moment. "I have a couple of things to say to you, and I hope at the end, you will still call me yours."

Kirsten was expecting to hear about what she already knew. She wondered how he would explain it and how she would still want to be with him. Over the last year, Kirsten couldn't deny the strength of her love for Gabriel and the bond that she and Allison shared. The recent events had happened so fast that Kirsten hadn't even had enough time to properly process it all, much less decide what to do about it.

Kirsten inhaled deep and nodded. "Tell me everything." She would need to act surprised and unaware if Gabriel revealed information about Allison, or the warehouse meeting she had seen. And as hard as it was to process, Kirsten would need to be open to the idea of staying with Gabriel, at least for now.

Gabriel shifted a bit to get comfortable and began, "I am not a good man, Kirsten. I… I have done things, and I am doing things to help further my career." He paused for a moment before continuing. "And it is because of this that I realize I have enemies, and those even that I thought I could trust can turn against me."

Gabriel leaned back, and Kirsten shifted to get more comfortable as he went on. "Allison was a part of our work and then used that information to blackmail me into doing something for her."

"What was it?" Kirsten asked. She was internally bracing herself for the inevitable response.

"She had me cheat on you with her. Twice," Gabriel said. He was choking up a bit while saying it. Kirsten turned away. She knew this information was coming, but hearing it come out of Gabriel's mouth made the wound just as fresh as seeing it happen again for the first time. Tears started falling down her face. She was hurt, sad, and angry all at once.

As Kirsten turned back to face Gabriel, she could see he was also crying, and his eyes, his damn eyes, took Kirsten in and looked so loving and regretful. Gabriel attempted to reach out and grab Kirsten's hand but hesitated as he got closer and pulled it back. "I'm so sorry," he said again, resting his hand back in his lap.

Kirsten leaned forward and grabbed his hand in hers. "I believe you," she said softly. "Tell me the rest."

Gabriel calmed somewhat as Kirsten held his hand. He cleared his throat and continued speaking. "I co-run smuggling operations in this area with some other men. The ones you met at the fundraiser when we first met. This is not a clean job, as people often get hurt and/or killed in the process."

Kirsten didn't move, slightly shocked, but as she thought for a moment, she started to put the pieces together and asked, "Smuggle what?"

"Various items and merchandise for ourselves and other clients," Gabriel said. "Allison was a part of this as well, and at some point, she turned and blackmailed me by threatening to reveal this information to you unless I did what she asked."

"So why tell me now?" Kirsten asked. She was speaking more precisely this time as she was recovering from the initial shock of it all. She knew that something illegal must've been going on, or otherwise Mr Fox wouldn't be watching. However, Kirsten's feelings and what she knew of Gabriel up to this point softened that blow, and she wasn't as turned off by it as she thought she would've been. "What changed?"

"You remember that surprise I was going to share with you on the yacht?" Gabriel began. Kirsten nodded.

"I was going to tell you then about my real job and ask that you be a part of it." Gabriel adjusted more in his seat as he continued. "I want you; I want… to protect you. I want you by my side. I've known for some time that I want you. I just needed to be sure that you wanted it too and that I could trust you with the information."

"I do love you, and I want to be with you," Kirsten said as she sat back and let go of Gabriel's hand. Gabriel's face brightened a bit but sank again, wondering what Kirsten was going to follow with.

"But I can't while Allison is still around," Kirsten said. She then explained what happened with her and Allison the night prior. Kirsten was careful not to let on with information about what she saw but only gave info on what Allison said and the fight that ensued afterward. Kirsten said that if she could even heal from the emotional trauma, Allison couldn't be around her or Gabriel.

"I'm sorry you went through that," Gabriel started to say. "I don't know what got into her. But I agree, and I've already spoken to the other members, and collectively we spoke to Allison and dismissed her from our service."

Kirsten nodded but was puzzled and leaned forward to ask, "Aren't you afraid she'll talk?"

"No," Gabriel said quickly. "She was paid for her part and will move to join one of our partners on the west coast."

Kirsten nodded but didn't say anything. After a moment of silence, Gabriel got up to leave. As he stood there by the couch, he glanced down at Kirsten, who was looking up at him. "I know it's a lot to take in," he said. "I hope you can find it in you to forgive me if nothing else. I love you, and I always will, even if you decide to leave," Gabriel finished and headed to the door.

Gabriel turned to look at Kirsten one last time before opening the door to leave. As he stepped out the door, he felt a tug on his arm. Gabriel stopped and turned around. Kirsten was there with tears in her eyes. Before Gabriel could speak, Kirsten leaned forward and kissed him.

"I forgive you," Kirsten said softly, still holding his face in her hands. Her brain was swimming. She wanted to forgive him but didn't want it to be so easy.

Gabriel smiled, and after a pause, just said, "Thank you." He turned to leave again, but Kirsten grabbed his arm. Gabriel turned to look back. Kirsten's eyes met his; they were full of love and compassion. Kirsten couldn't let him go. She wanted him. No, she needed him.

"Stay," was all Kirsten said. So soft and welcoming that it took a moment for Gabriel to process the statement. Kirsten pulled harder at his arm, and Gabriel stepped back into the apartment just enough to close the door behind him with his free hand. Kirsten stepped in close and came up to kiss him. Gabriel met her as she did, and the two locked together in each other's arms.

Tears fell from both as they continued to hold each other. After several minutes, Kirsten relaxed and led Gabriel to her room. The two continued for some time before they snuggled up to each other and fell asleep.

Kirsten, although still upset inside, had relaxed a lot and came to terms with what happened. She knew what Gabriel was doing was wrong, and she was aware that Mr Fox was watching now. But she didn't care. She loved Gabriel and feeling his body next to hers even as he just disclosed what he did earlier that evening. She felt safe and closer to him than ever before now that she knew the truth about everything.

Kirsten's phone buzzed a few times. She and Gabriel were still asleep when Kirsten finally woke up and reached over to grab it. 'Missed call from unknown.' Kirsten rolled her eyes and let out an exacerbated sigh. Mr Fox probably changed his number again.

Kirsten rolled over to her side, facing away from Gabriel, who was stirring on his side just waking up. Checking her phone, Kirsten saw that it was one thirty p.m.... Dang, she thought, must've needed that sleep. As Kirsten lay there looking at her phone, she found it hard to get comfortable as the pain from the fight still lingered. Her head hurt again, but she wasn't sure if it was from the fight yet, or just a random headache. She wasn't sure when she and Gabriel passed out, she had lost track of time while they were talking.

Kirsten's phone vibrated again. Same unknown caller, "Hello," Kirsten answered quietly. Gabriel shifted again next to her. Kirsten glanced over her shoulder to see if he was awake. Gabriel's eyes were still shut, and his breathing was quiet and normal. Kirsten figured he was still asleep but didn't want to chance it, so she carefully got up and left the room. As she got up, she noticed her head was throbbing harder than before. So the steps were slow going as she was rubbing her temples with one hand with her phone in the other as she walked.

As Kirsten got out into the central part of her apartment, the caller was already speaking though she wasn't listening as she was careful not to disturb Gabriel as she got out into the living room. She spoke again, "Hey, can you repeat that. I had to step away, so I didn't disturb Gabriel."

"I have some information that you will want to know," said the voice on the other end of the line.

"Mr Fox?" Kirsten questioned. "What's up?"

"Yes," came his voice through the phone. "Local PD found Allison's car in a ditch on her way out of town." He paused before continuing. "She's dead."

# Chapter 15

# Funeral

Dead? Kirsten was frozen for a moment as she processed the information she was just told. She had to admit that she was happy that she wouldn't be interfering with her and Gabriel any more. However, Kirsten wasn't thrilled that Allison was dead either. Conflicting thoughts and emotions came and went as Kirsten stood in her living room. Mr Fox was still on the phone, though he was quiet for a moment waiting for Kirsten to process this new development.

"Are you going to be okay?" Mr Fox finally asked. Kirsten snapped out of her thoughts and quickly answered back in agreement.

"Let me know when the funeral is," Kirsten said. She had realized while she said that that she honestly didn't have a clue as to how she would know about any funeral arrangements. She and Allison had been friends for a year and had only ever just spoken about each other's family. Kirsten wasn't sure if Allison's family even knew about her, let alone would make sure she got information on her death. If it hadn't been for Mr Fox's involvement now, Kirsten most likely wouldn't have ever known that Alison was dead.

"I will. I'll be in touch," Mr Fox said before hanging up the phone on his end. *Some pieces aren't fitting together,* Mr Fox thought as he sat in his office. Since that night, some things hadn't made sense when he was listening to the conference meeting with Kirsten. How was Kirsten "chosen"? And then the information he got from the agent sent to the warehouse that night seemed incomplete in light of the recent developments. Then there was this supposed mole to deal with that was apparently working with Allison. After a moment's pause, he grabbed his desk phone and dialed a number. "Yes," he said in greeting. "Meet me in my office. We need to talk."

Meanwhile, Kirsten had put her phone down and sat on her couch. After everything that Allison did just now, Kirsten found it more than challenging to feel any sense of genuine sadness or loss with Allison's death. Had this accident happened a few weeks ago, Kirsten might have felt differently about losing her close friend. Still, though, the shock of it happening was enough to make Kirsten take a pause and reflect on her life for a bit.

Kirsten was still lost in thought when she felt a hand touch her shoulder. She jumped slightly, though it felt more intense in her chest. Kirsten turned and put her hand on her chest as she relaxed and breathed deep a few times. Realizing it was just Gabriel, Kirsten calmed quickly. "Hey, love," he said as he sat next to her. "Is everything all right?"

Kirsten nodded slightly as she leaned into his shoulder. "Yes... Well, kind of," she started to say.

Gabriel's facial expression changed to concern. "Tell me," he softly pleaded. Kirsten looked up into his eyes. He had a look of genuine concern in his eyes that moved Kirsten in her own heart.

Her eyes started to water a bit as she tried to speak. "Allison was found dead earlier today in a car accident." As Kirsten said the words out loud, she realized that she had more feelings about what happened than she initially realized. Full tears never actually came, but Kirsten did notice that in combination with her eyes watering, her throat choked up a bit after speaking.

Gabriel didn't say anything in response and just brought Kirsten in closer and hugged her. The two sat embraced in the hug for several minutes in silence before finally separating. Gabriel and Kirsten looked at each other for a moment longer before Gabriel finally spoke. "Are you going to be all right?"

Kirsten nodded and said yes. She explained her internal dilemma about what happened with Allison and their past year of friendship prior. Gabriel listened intently as Kirsten verbally processed her emotions while talking.

When they had finished, the couple showered and cleaned up. Only to spend the rest of the day just enjoying each other's company in Kirsten's place. The next few days were uneventful as some sense of normalcy came back into Kirsten's life. It was strange not to hear from Allison at all despite the rough ending. The texts and times they got together were such a part of Kirsten's routine that even though she was happy not to have that stress or drama any more, she was still indifferent about losing Allison completely.

Kirsten and Gabriel's relationship, however, remained steady, even increased. Over the last few days together, Kirsten and Gabriel had grown closer again, and as Gabriel would disclose small portions of his work to her, Kirsten became more accepting of his role in this venture, and her role, at his side.

That following week, Kirsten went to work and put in her two weeks' notice. She and Gabriel had decided she would play a more prominent role in his business in time. So, to begin this, Kirsten needed to be free from her regular job. She had discussed with Gabriel about moving in together at some point soon. Once they worked out her finances, she decided to quit.

Mr Fox had been strangely silent the last few days since the notification of Allison's death. The only other message she received from him was more recent, and it was just details of Allison's funeral. Kirsten noted the date in her calendar and didn't think much about Mr Fox's absent behavior. No news must be good news, she thought.

Allison's funeral was small. Kirsten only recognized a handful of individuals from the company Allison worked for. It was a closed casket service since they had said that her face was severely damaged in the car accident when she hit the steering wheel before flying through the windshield. Gabriel and Kirsten sat in the back. Neither one knew what the other did regarding the final moments leading up to Allison's death.

Kirsten had to pretend to only know what Gabriel told her about what happened before she and Allison got into their huge fight in Allison's apartment. Gabriel likewise had to play ignorant of any information about Allison after that altercation with Kirsten took place. Together they both sat in silence in the church pew throughout the service.

Both Kirsten and Gabriel were in the classic black funeral attire. However, Kirsten had taken her new position with Gabriel to the next level. She was now adorned with designer clothes and accessories. It was a simple outfit, but you would see that it was expensive if you knew the brand names and jewelry. Kirsten sat upright and rigid. She sat with the attitude of someone who was above the rest and only there for pity's sake.

Gabriel sat the same. With Kirsten at his side now more in the know about what he did and supporting it, Gabriel didn't have to hide any more. Kirsten followed suit. If she was to be his queen and help him run his empire, she would need to fit in better and be taken more seriously by his coworkers.

Kirsten was second in command now, and with Allison gone, however it happened, it was irrelevant. Kirsten missed the past times but suppressed those memories as she embraced her new life with Gabriel.

At the cemetery, Kirsten and Gabriel stood close and towards the back. Both looked on as though they had knowledge and secrets about what happened, which was true, but not revealed. Those who saw them just took them for other casual friends of Allison. The sun beat down; Gabriel had sunglasses on that hid his eyes well. He didn't want them to give away his lack of empathy. Kirsten had a pair of her own on for the same reason.

After the service, Gabriel and Kirsten walked back to their car quickly. As they approached the vehicle, Kirsten noticed a few people standing some distance off in another part of the cemetery. Initially, she glanced over and shrugged them off as just some others paying respects to someone else. But something seemed strange to Kirsten for some reason, and so she kept an eye in that direction as they pulled away.

Driving slow out of the cemetery, Gabriel followed the road around to the exit. As he did so, Kirsten noticed that she would get a better look at the people she had seen earlier, and so she fixed her eyes on their position. The tinted windows of the car kept her staring inconspicuously at those outside the vehicle. As they got closer, Kirsten could see three men standing around a stone. Two of them were standing, and one was kneeling. As if to be reading, whatever was written on the gravestone they were near.

Kirsten looked harder as she got closer to the men's position. As they drove closer, she noticed that it was Mr Fox kneeling there. The other two must be members of his team, she thought. She shouldn't have been surprised to see him there, considering his involvement with Allison and Gabriel, but since she hadn't heard from him for almost a week now, Kirsten thought that perhaps some priorities had changed. Or maybe she wished they had or hoped? It was hard for her to decipher her thoughts and feelings. She was ready and willing to embrace her life with Gabriel more fully. And she probably would if it wasn't for Mr Fox's involvement.

Mr Fox noticed Kirsten and Gabriel driving past. He knew it was them though he couldn't see in the vehicle. He didn't need to see to know that Kirsten was watching. As Kirsten passed his position, Mr Fox stood up and turned to face the men he was with. "We need to keep a closer eye on the developments going forward."

"Are you going to inform Kirsten?" one asked.

"No," Mr Fox responded. "She will play her part better in ignorance to our movements. Besides, I need more information before I speak to Kirsten again."

"What of the mole?" the other asked.

"He has fooled us for the last time," Mr Fox said solemnly. He glanced towards Allison's gravesite; some people were still lingering as she was lowered down, and others, like Kirsten and Gabriel, made a hasty departure. Mr Fox was concerned as he paused in thought before continuing, "Bring him in for interrogation. Hopefully, he won't be missed until I get what I need from him." Then, turning back to face the man who asked the question, said, "And by then, it won't matter."

The men turned collectively to walk away. Mr Fox spoke again: "The first major chess move has been played," he began. "We need to get three moves ahead."

*... A few weeks later*

Kirsten was going through some things in her apartment. She

was getting ready to move in with Gabriel, so she threw some things away and was packing others. The last few weeks had been relatively smooth, Mr Fox had been quiet, and with Allison gone, Kirsten's life came to a screeching halt. She hadn't realized how much of her free time and attention was being taken by both Allison and Mr Fox. Of course, there was Gabriel, but that was time that Kirsten enjoyed spending.

*BEEP! BEEP!*

Kirsten went to grab her phone. She always got a weird feeling when she would hear a text message now. With Allison gone, Mr Fox silent, and Kirsten spending more time with Gabriel, her phone went off considerably less each day. It shouldn't've bothered her as much as it did, but she couldn't help the feeling of fear of 'what now' when her phone would ring.

*'Meet at the Ocean Sands Hotel, room 334.'* — *Unknown*

Kirsten paused for a moment before responding. The last time she was in that room sent her on an emotional rollercoaster that she did not want to repeat. Thinking more, she remembered that Gabriel was meeting some possible clients downtown and that his office was empty today. No further messages appeared as Kirsten stood there. It must not be an emergency, she thought. Perhaps it would just be a casual update since he had been absent for a while. It was probably going to be a general debrief of the events thus far.

*'What time?'* — *Kirsten*

*'As soon as possible.'* — *Unknown*

"Ugh," Kirsten said, exhaling heavily. She had hoped that Mr Fox would've just allowed her to fall off the radar. Kirsten paused again before responding. She wasn't ready for another wave of bad news leading to worse, between what happened with Gabriel and Allison, then Allison's death, and now working for and aligning herself more with Gabriel. Kirsten was ready just to disappear.

*'Give me twenty minutes.' — Kirsten*

*'I'll be waiting.' — Unknown*

Kirsten took her time getting ready and heading over. Hypothetical thoughts and scenarios raced through her mind. She didn't know what was coming. Maybe, she didn't want to know. Either way, she knew in the back of her mind that at some point, she was going to have to face this reality.

*Knock, knock!*

Mr Fox opened the door promptly and let Kirsten in. The room was emptier this time, and instead of the team of several people, only two were present in the room with Mr Fox. He led Kirsten into the other half of the room where the scope was set up the last time she was here. This time, however, just a table and a laptop with some headphones and binoculars.

The other two men stayed where they were near the door. They each had a laptop and earpieces in. Both gave little notice to Kirsten's presence as she walked through with Mr Fox. The curtains were still drawn most of the way, and only some of the lights were used. Mr Fox motioned for Kirsten to sit down across from him at the table and sat down himself.

"I apologize for not staying in constant update with you as I had been before," Mr Fox began. "Some things we heard that night here when you were with me before Allison died didn't sit right with me, and I needed to do more investigating."

Kirsten just sat quietly for a moment, waiting to make sure he was done speaking. When Mr Fox didn't continue, Kirsten asked, "So what have you found out?"

Mr Fox sat back in his chair. "First," he said quickly. "First, tell me what Gabriel has revealed to you since that night that

Allison died."

Kirsten was taken aback at first. She just assumed that Mr Fox was aware of everything she knew. But this would mean that either he had some information that he needed more pieces for. Or, he wanted to know what lies had been said so he could clarify them as they come out. Kirsten was hesitant to reveal too much until she knew more about what Mr Fox was already planning.

Mr Fox could tell she was hesitating, so he just started speaking. "Kirsten, you'll notice that my team is considerably smaller." Kirsten nodded as he continued, "I discovered that Allison was in contact with someone on my team, and he was feeding her information about what we were doing."

Kirsten straightened up in her seat. Concern spread across her face. "So what does that mean for me?"

"We found the mole and have… extracted some information from him." Mr Fox paused before he went on. "Allison knew the whole time. You were her target back in the gym when you first met."

Kirsten's face switched from concern to shock and disbelief. Mr Fox went on to explain that the group was already on to them before Kirsten was involved. And that through the mole, Allison was watching Kirsten for a few days before she made contact. "Allison then purposefully pulled you into their inner circle. Why and what for? I don't have those answers yet," Mr Fox finished.

"So what do you need me to do now?" Kirsten asked.

Mr Fox spun his laptop to face Kirsten. The screen showed a picture of one of the men Kirsten saw both at the warehouse some time ago and in Gabriel's office during the meeting she observed from this room. Kirsten stared at the screen for a moment before glancing back up at Mr Fox with a confused and questioning look.

"This is Mr Thompson," Mr Fox said plainly. "He is from out of state but always gets the same room at the Hotel Bravada near the harbor. I need a listening device put in his room, as well as a camera if possible." Kirsten started to protest, but Mr Fox put his finger up to silence her until he finished speaking. "He is closest to Gabriel, other than you. And with Allison and the mole gone, I need a way to get more information." Mr Fox paused as he finished.

"Sooo?" Kirsten questioned. She could most definitely just use her relationship with Gabriel to get information and give it back to Mr Fox. Why he was pushing on this now with one of Gabriel's associates, Kirsten wasn't sure.

"I can't trust everyone," Mr Fox explained. "That's why you only see the two men here now. I can't be sure that more aren't possibly compromised." Mr Fox got up and reached into a bag on the floor near the wall. He pulled out a small pouch and handed it to Kirsten. In it, she found several listening devices and a camera. All of it was relatively small and easily concealable.

Kirsten realized exactly what Mr Fox was asking. "You want me to plant the bugs?" she asked almost sarcastically. Mr Fox only nodded in agreement and said nothing.

Kirsten exhaled heavily through her nose. She was going to ask how he expected her to do that. But she already knew the answer. She would be expected to figure it out. Mr Fox never cared how someone accomplished a task only that it was accomplished and to the standards he set. Kirsten closed up the bag and rested it in her lap.

Mr Fox turned the laptop back to face him and then wrote down the hotel's address and room number that Mr Thompson stayed in and slid it across the table to Kirsten's position. "Where is he now?" Kirsten asked, taking the paper and reading it over.

"With Gabriel in the meeting downtown."

And with that, Kirsten got up to leave. Mr Fox followed her to the door and let her out. Once she was gone, one of the other men in the room asked, "You think she's flipped?"

Mr Fox shook his head. "No. Not yet." He walked over to the window and glanced down over the front of the hotel. After a few minutes of awkward silence, he noticed Kirsten walking out to her car. "But if we are to stay ahead, then we must act like it's a possibility," he finished.

Mr Fox was still looking out the window as the other men nodded to each other. "Go to the warehouse," he said, turning back to face them in the room. "If you can, go in and investigate what may or may not be there."

The two men got up and prepared to leave. "What will you do?" the one asked.

Mr Fox thought for a moment before answering. "I'm going to go back through the call and email logs from Gabriel's trip in Vegas going forward. I think we missed something."

# Chapter 16

# New Evidence

Kirsten arrived at the address given to her by Mr Fox. She parked and stared off for a moment. The whole ride there, she was contemplating whether or not to even go through with it. She knew that she needed to, she knew that she should, but she didn't want to.

Kirsten's life had changed drastically in the last few weeks since she agreed to be with Gabriel and help with his venture. She had taken over Allison's position and then some. Access to various accounts and shipping manifests through the company and the inside information on the extra cargo brought in and the legitimate freight. Kirsten answered directly and only to Gabriel, and the rest of the members understood that she was there to help oversee the parts of the operation that Gabriel couldn't do on his own.

For Kirsten, this meant a considerable increase in cash flow. Since beginning to work for Gabriel, she upgraded her car, wardrobe and was soon to move in with Gabriel at his condo at the end of the month coming shortly. At first, Kirsten didn't care about the extra stuff; she had grown up average middle class, and while more money and things were nice to have, she wasn't necessarily impressed by them. That said, if she were to fit in and play the part, then she would have to live as these people did.

Kirsten snapped out of her thoughts and got out of her car,

and looked around. The building was a modest condominium complex. Each condo on each floor had a balcony with sliding doors. Kirsten had the devices Mr Fox had given her in her small bag that she had slung over her shoulder.

After walking on the ground floor, Kirsten noticed that the elevator was similar to Gabriel's place. You needed a key to access particular floors since the elevators on each side of the building went directly to the condos. The stairs were open and must be generally used for maintenance and emergencies because while the main floor was unlocked, each door going up was locked with a unique lock that only fire and rescue or building staff would have. The doors could be opened without the key to utilize the stairs when leaving the building from the condos in an emergency. Kirsten looked around more to decide how to best approach it.

Kirsten looked at the nameplate near the main door. Here she could see which side of the building her target's room was and verified the room number. Next to the name was a buzzer which she assumed was to alert the occupant of a visitor on the ground floor. After some more thought, she headed to the roof via the emergency stairs. Thankfully, the roof door was locked with a standard doorknob lock, and it was quickly picked.

Once on the roof, Kirsten looked around. The roof was your basic commercial roof; tar paper and pea gravel layers and HVAC machines staggered about. Kirsten walked closer to the edge and glanced over. The building was at least twenty floors. She didn't have any rope with her, but that might be too obvious and draw some unwanted attention on second thought.

Glancing over the railing on the edge of the building, Kirsten looked down again and contemplated how best to go about this. Each balcony was open, directly above it, and had a metal railing around the outside edge. Kirsten glanced around at the ground below. No one was in the vicinity. She then glanced around the side of the building. No one was currently outside on their balconies on this side of the building.

So, ever so casually, Kirsten stood back up, grabbed the railing and flipped over it. Facing the building while she gripped the railing, using her feet braced against the building, Kirsten then dropped, free-falling until she caught the first balcony railing. Hanging over the edge, Kirsten glanced down as she let go and fell to the next floor catching herself again on the balcony railing.

Kirsten continued this for a few more floors until she reached the one she needed. Then, pulling herself up over the railing and onto the balcony, Kirsten, very casually, approached the sliding door. It wasn't locked. Kirsten breathed a sigh of relief and entered the condo carefully.

The layout was very minimalist and modern. Much to be expected of a temporary second home of a well-financed individual. Kirsten placed the listening devices as close to the key spots that were the best places to catch conversations. Then she put the cameras inside the vents.

Afterward, she wiped off the surfaces that she touched, and with great care, making sure everything was exactly like it was when she came in, Kirsten then left out via the elevator and exited the building. After reaching her car, Kirsten texted Mr Fox.

*'Everything is in place.' — Kirsten*

Kirsten didn't wait for a response. She wasn't too concerned about it. Mr Fox would undoubtedly test his video and sound equipment and verify that the locations would work and that everything functioned normally. She didn't need to wait around for that. So, after putting her phone away, Kirsten drove back home to continue sorting through her things.

Mr Fox was in his office when he received Kirsten's text. Stacks of papers were around him, and he was currently looking at something on his laptop when the phone buzzed next to him. He didn't respond to Kirsten's update. Partly because he didn't need to, and partly because he was trying to limit his communication with Kirsten to better protect her from being discovered.

Once he read the message, he returned to his laptop, punched some keys, and pulled up the video footage of Mr Thompson's place. After reviewing that and the audio connection, he started to record. Mr Fox had been going through the phone calls and texts of Gabriel, Allison and Kirsten in the days leading up to Vegas through the time of Allison's death.

During his first run-through, Mr Fox noticed some texts and calls from Allison and Mr Thompson right before Gabriel left for Vegas. He saved these to go back over again later as he continued through the main lines of communication going forward. Then, he noticed two phone calls from Allison to Gabriel the night she died, which pinged his memory. He knew of Allison's fight with Kirsten and that she was at the warehouse before the accident. Thinking more, Mr Fox then picked up his desk phone and dialed some numbers. After a brief moment of ringing, a man answered on the other end.

"Get me Allison Brown's autopsy," Mr Fox said after the greeting. "I have a hunch, but I need more information." A woman's voice came through the phone on the other end.

"Thank you," Mr Fox said as he hung up.

He sat back in his chair and thought some more. He was finally putting some pieces together, and he didn't like where it was going. He went back to the papers, and as he was browsing, again, he suddenly had another thought. It was a long shot, but something might prove useful and hopefully solve the puzzle.

Mr Fox grabbed his phone again and dialed a number. "Can you get me the autopsy of an individual in Vegas?" he asked. "Yes, hold on a minute," he said as he shuffled through some of the papers on his desk. "Yes, here. A Mr Jeffery Thomas, May 18$^{th}$." Another pause as the man on the phone spoke. "Yes. Thank you so much," Mr Fox finished.

It would be a waiting game for a few days while those reports made it to his desk. In the meantime, he continued to go through the paperwork. Now, however, he was focused on the Allison and Mr Thompson conversations. He needed more pieces, and he hoped it would come in time before it was too late.

A few days later, Mr Fox was in his office again when he got a knock on the door. "Come in," he called out. In walked a female with a lab coat on over her business attire, her I.D. badge was clipped to the collar, in one hand, she held a thick folder, in the other, a tablet. She walked with purpose and haste as she approached the desk.

Handing the papers to Mr Fox, she then took the tablet in both hands and began to pull up something on it. Mr Fox took the folder and began to look through the papers. "Did you find anything?" he asked, keeping his gaze on the documents in his hands.

"Possibly," the woman said.

"Show me."

The woman turned the tablet to face Mr Fox and proceeded to explain. "You'll see in the folder, but here is a close-up of the head injury," she began. "The primary contusion is a good match for what happened in her vehicle. Un-seat-belted, and at her speed, her head would've smashed the steering wheel and then as she was launched forward through the windshield; we can see the second part of the impact in the top of her head with the lacerations from the glass."

"So, we are looking at a legitimate car accident?" Mr Fox interrupted.

"Not quite. I wouldn't have bothered to check further had you not requested it," the woman said. "But since I was, I saw that her blood alcohol level was pretty high. However, her stomach was reported to be empty. Which means that either…"

"She is such a lightweight, and her metabolism is shit that the alcohol stayed that high in her system long after she finished her last drink and then managed to fight Kirsten. And drive to the warehouse fine before driving again and crashing. Or… She was injected so the reports would reflect alcohol content so it would appear that she was drunk, and the accident would be dismissed," Mr Fox finished her statement for her as he put the pieces together.

The woman nodded in acknowledgment after he finished speaking. "I came to the same conclusion, so I looked further. Because for her to have that system reading, she would have to be alive so the heart would pump it through her system," she said as she was swiping at the screen of the tablet again. "So first, I checked her for a puncture wound, and I think I found one here," she said as she faced the tablet to Mr Fox again. "Ever so small and would've continued to go unnoticed if I hadn't been looking for it. I wish I still had her body to verify."

"Anything else?" Mr Fox asked.

"Possibly, yes. Some unusual bruising in the chest area, but again, this is difficult to make out since I don't have her body anymore," she said.

"Go on."

The woman pulled up another photo on the tablet and zoomed in. "See here. These bruises don't line up with her hitting the steering wheel in her accident," she said, pointing to a small area to the left of the sternum. "See, the bruising up near her clavicle matches the impact in the car. And again, I would've associated these bruises with that as well, or the fight she had prior. However, if someone injected her after she died, they would've needed to pump her chest rather roughly to get the blood to move a bit. Additionally, those bruises wouldn't go away because she was already dead."

Mr Fox continued to look at the screen in front of him for a moment before responding. "So, if I understand correctly. We possibly have evidence that Allison was killed before the crash. Possibly, by blunt force trauma to the head. She was possibly injected in the neck with a synthetic alcohol substance and possibly had it "pumped" through her system manually. Then possibly, put in the car and sent off to make it look like an accident."

The woman nodded, affirming Mr Fox's summary. She took the tablet back in her hand and stood for a moment. Mr Fox sat back in his chair before standing and walking to the window. Glancing out, he pondered a moment and then turned back to the woman. "Too many possibilities for concrete evidence," he started to say. "I have more information coming. When it gets here, I'll have you look it over like you did this one. Hopefully, we can find a connection."

And with that, the woman left. Mr Fox sat back down at his desk and continued looking through the folder and reviewing the autopsy reports. "Hopefully," he muttered to himself quietly.

# Chapter 17

# The Big Picture

*Part 1 — Mr Fox*

It had been a few more days since Mr Fox had discovered possible foul play with Allison's death. He hadn't received any reports from when Gabriel had been in Vegas yet, but an email he received just the day prior assured him it was incoming. In the meantime, Mr Fox had been going through the various reports trying to find more information on why Kirsten was chosen for what purpose.

It would prove to be a long and tedious process, however. Mr Fox had been going line by line for several days now, and it all seemed to blur together. He had been working on this operation for over a year, and now, he was closer than ever. But he needed more concrete connections to get everyone involved.

Kirsten had been successful in planting the listening bugs in Mr Thompsons' place. However, in the days that followed, there wasn't much more than casual chatter heard there. Kirsten was now living with Gabriel at his place, which was confirmed by the bugs planted there. Three new shipments had come in, and much to Mr Fox's disappointment, he wasn't able to move on them yet. However, there was a new shipment arriving, and hopefully, with Kirsten's help, he could finally bring this operation to a close.

The mole that Allison was using seemed only to be partly helpful. He didn't know much about the long-term plans. Clever on their part, to not disclose the plans beyond the immediate need, that way if he got caught, as he did, he wouldn't be of much help beyond the information that was past or current. Further questioning of the mole revealed that the intel he gave to Allison was minimal after Kirsten was discovered. A few pieces of her movements and conversations with Mr Fox were revealed, but nothing significant about the overall plan.

This information brought Mr Fox to the conclusion that he was only needed to keep them a step ahead and not concerned about deterring the operation altogether. At the present time, Mr Fox couldn't decide if that was smart or cocky. And despite his best efforts, the mole either didn't know or was sealed shut on any information about what Kirsten was needed for. The obvious thing was to use her as leverage or as a double agent. Neither of which was favorable to Mr Fox or his operation.

Gabriel hadn't asked to see, nor were there any check-ins with the mole. So, Mr Fox let him sit in custody to continue to watch him until something, if anything, came up where he was needed again.

At this time now, Mr Fox had finished the main portion of his piling paperwork that directly related to Allison and Gabriel's phone chatter. Now, he was turning his attention to the text messages between Allison and Mr Thompson. It was nearing the end of the day now, and Mr Fox noticed that he was the only one left in his office. The sun was setting outside his window as he leaned back in his chair and rubbed his eyes. It had been a rough, few days; mentally, he was drained.

He got up to stretch his legs and leaned over his desk. And then, he saw it. A few of the messages between Allison and Mr Thompson right after Gabriel left for Vegas. As Mr Fox read them, his jaw tightened. He grabbed his phone and quickly dialed. "Hey!" he said sharply. "I've got another piece of the puzzle; we need to move quickly. Meet me at the hotel room." He finished speaking, grabbed his laptop and headed out.

As he was about to leave, his email notification went off on his phone. Mr Fox checked it quickly. It was the autopsy and crime details of the Vegas incident with Jeffery Thomas. This caused Mr Fox to stop in his tracks and turn back to his desk. He grabbed the desk phone and dialed a number. "Hello," he greeted then continued, "Yes, I know it's getting late. But I just received the files from Vegas. If I forward them to you, can you look them over and get back to me?"

There was a murmur of agreement in the earpiece. And with that, Mr Fox hung up and quickly forwarded the email to his M.E. As he left the building, Mr Fox smiled to himself. The puzzle was becoming more apparent, and the pieces were moving in his favor for now. He has been doing this job for far too long to jump for joy just yet. But at this moment, Mr Fox felt a sense of comfort knowing that this operation would be finally coming to a close.

As Mr Fox headed to the hotel, he was replaying the pieces over in his head, trying to see if anything else made sense and if he had all the pieces he needed. One of the mystery players was Kirsten. Mr Fox still didn't know what their plan was for her. The obvious answer, of course, came from the conversation he overheard that night when he had Kirsten with him in the hotel. Gabriel had mentioned that he wanted to "flip" her, and have Kirsten join him.

On the surface, this seemed bad. However, it was a bit problematic since Kirsten wouldn't flip entirely. At least, not of her own volition. Something would have to be drastic and wrong for Kirsten to flip like that. The more Mr Fox thought about it, the more uneasy he became. The details of Allison's death and this new information led Mr Fox to believe that Kirsten may be in big trouble if he didn't play his next moves correctly.

For now, however, he wasn't going to show his cards. If something got out about what he knew too soon or before he was ready to move in, it could be catastrophic not just for Kirsten but also for his team. Mr Fox pulled up to the hotel that he had been using as a remote operating center.

He pulled into the hotel parking lot and walked up to the room. The walk to the room was slower than usual. More plans and thoughts weighed on his mind. As he entered the room, Mr Fox was greeted by the two men he'd stayed close to during the last few weeks of the operation.

"What's the development?" the first one asked as Mr Fox put his things down on the table.

Mr Fox then explained the details of Allison's autopsy and his suspicions about Gabriel's trip to Vegas. "I'm still waiting for Lindsey to get back to me with what she can find with that autopsy." He paused for a moment as he finished.

"We have some development as well," said the second man pulling some paperwork out of a folder on the desk.

"What's this?" Mr Fox asked as he took the papers from him.

"Shipping manifests for the next shipment coming in through Gabriel's docks," he replied.

Mr Fox ran through the paperwork for a few minutes as he asked, "Anything unusual?"

"This time, yes," the man said as he reached over to point at the block on the last page.

Mr Fox grew tense as he looked over the sheet. "This is the first time he's tried to move anything like this," he said anxiously. The men nodded in agreement. "Does Kirsten know?"

"Not yet that we can tell," the men almost spoke in unison, acknowledging the unknown answer together.

Mr Fox put the papers down on the table, glancing back over the first one. "When is this one due to arrive?" he asked as he glanced over the papers looking for the date himself.

"Next week," the first man replied.

"I thought I had more time," Mr Fox muttered under his breath to himself.

"Sir?" the second man asked.

"Nothing." Mr Fox snapped out of his thoughts. Then he remembered the other piece of information he had to share and went to his bag. "Here," he said, pulling a stack of papers out of his bag. "Here are the transcripts of the conversation between Allison and Mr Thompson. These were dated the day Gabriel was in Vegas."

The men took the pages from Mr Fox and shared them between themselves. After reading the conversation, both men looked up at Mr Fox and handed him back the papers. Their faces showed a small sign of shock as they adjusted themselves in their seats.

"Do we tell Kirsten?" the first one asked.

"Not yet," Mr Fox answered as he put the papers back in his bag. "We do, however, need to tell Kirsten about this shipment, and we have to…" He paused as he felt his phone vibrate in his pocket. After pulling it out and seeing who the caller was, he quickly answered. "Yes?"

After a few moments of listening, Mr Fox's expression changed, and he was hardly holding in his excitement. "Yes," he almost shouted as he got up and went to open his laptop. "Send me everything… Thank you so much, Lindsay."

Mr Fox hung up and turned to his men. "Check."

The men jumped slightly in their seats. "What's next?" the second man asked quickly.

"We get Kirsten to have a meeting," Mr Fox said as he went back to his phone and sent Kirsten a text. "How we play this next part will determine if we can get the whole operation at once. One big checkmate."

*'The weather looks rough the next few days.'* — Mr Fox
*'How bad do you think it'll be?'* — Kirsten
*'Ocean Sands Hotel. Room 334. One hour.'* — Mr Fox

Part 2 — Kirsten

Kirsten had just finished unpacking the last of her things into Gabriel's place. Thankfully, they didn't have an excessive number of things between the two of them, so the condo still seemed very spacious.

Although, to be fair, Kirsten only brought her clothes and personal items when she moved. Since Gabriel already had a fully stocked kitchen and plenty of furniture, she didn't need to get anything other than what she brought. This also made moving easy, just a few trips in her car.

Gabriel had been tied up at work today, but it gave Kirsten time to properly finish unpacking and settle in better. At the same time, Kirsten was in email correspondence with Mr Thompson and the future customer about the upcoming shipments. It had been a relatively smooth process getting into the swing of things with Gabriel and his work.

After responding to Mr Fox's text, Kirsten quickly cleaned up and got ready to leave. As she did, she noticed her head was slightly throbbing again. Nothing terrible, but enough to bother her. Once in her car, Kirsten put the top down and let the fresh summer air blow her hair and clear her head.

As she arrived at the hotel, Kirsten sat a moment in the car. She glanced up through her windshield up towards the room that she knew Mr Fox was in. She silently prayed that she wouldn't hear any more bad news. Secretly she hoped that the news would be to say that the operation was over and they got what they needed. Kirsten knew that wasn't the case, but the thought of hope in the matter was all she was looking for. She just wanted to be with Gabriel and left alone.

Breathing a heavy exhale, Kirsten finally got out of the car and headed up to the room. When she got there, the door was opened almost on cue. As if she was being watched right up to the moment she stood there. Upon entering the room, she noticed it was the same two men that Mr Fox had previously had there. Mr Fox, of course, was sitting in the adjoining room at the table with his laptop open in front of him.

Kirsten came in and sat down across from Mr Fox as she had before. He didn't move to acknowledge her. Instead, he stared intently at his screen. Kirsten shifted a bit in her seat, waiting for him to finish whatever he was doing. And after a few awkward moments, Mr Fox finally looked up at Kirsten and smiled.

"Kirsten, I've been looking into Allison's death, and the details have me puzzled," Mr Fox said calmly.

"What do you mean?" Kirsten asked. She was curious but not interested in the details. Allison was dead to her, and as much as she missed the old times of their friendship, this was overshadowed by her betrayal to Kirsten with Gabriel.

"We found evidence of murder," Mr Fox began to explain. Kirsten's body language softened a bit.

Mr Fox explained how despite the fight she had with Allison, there was still some unusual bruising along with a toxicology report that didn't make sense. Some possible evidence suggested that a substance was injected and manually pumped through her system to look like she was intoxicated. Then the car accident was used to cover up those details.

Kirsten sat silent for a moment. She was thinking about whether or not she even cared that Allison was killed or just died on her own. But curiosity got the better of her, and she, as casually as possible, asked, "Who is your suspect?"

"Gabriel," Mr Fox said very sincerely.

Kirsten's heart sank a bit. She was worried that this was the reason he was explaining Allison's death details to her. Because he suspected Gabriel was directly involved. She had hoped it was going to be just a regular detail update this time. She should've known better; any information Mr Fox has found has led to one form of heartbreak or another through this process.

"What's your evidence?" Kirsten asked firmly. She was sure Mr Fox had some, and he wouldn't be talking to her if he didn't. But she needed to hear it from him to be certain herself.

"We found inconsistencies with the information given to us by the informant the night Allison arrived at the warehouse after your altercation. Additionally, I looked into Gabriel's Vegas trip. And I found that a Mr Jeffery Thomas was the man found dead in the hotel that Gabriel was brought in for questioning on," Mr Fox explained.

"And?"

"Mr Thomas died of the same M.O. as Allison. The only difference was the car accident that happened with him wasn't bad enough, and the unusual bruising and toxicology report were the same, so further investigation was warranted. However, it seems that Gabriel's lawyers found a loophole regarding the security footage at the hotel, which puts Gabriel in the vicinity around the time of death, but in no way could it be used to confirm that. So, he walked. And it seems he learned from that since Allison's was a much better cover-up." Mr Fox finished speaking as sat back in his chair as he let Kirsten process the information.

Kirsten didn't say anything. At first glance, one could dismiss the whole thing based on a lack of direct correlating evidence. But the more Kirsten thought the more it made sense. Gabriel had mentioned that he paid Allison her share and sent her to the west coast. But she remembers her car was found on a back road that didn't directly lead to the interstate.

Furthermore, once Kirsten was integrated into the systems with Gabriel's company, she noticed no notable withdrawal or payment made to Allison. Initially, Kirsten brushed it off and didn't think much of it. Now, though, she seemed more inclined to believe Mr Fox.

"So, what's our plan?" Kirsten finally asked solemnly.

"To hopefully use this to add to the list of charges as well as be able to move in when this shipment arrives," Mr Fox said as he put a few papers on the table in front of her.

Kirsten glanced down and scanned through the papers. Mr Fox waited patiently as Kirsten read through the documents. Why had she not seen this one? She recognized this shipping manifest since she was in charge of that part, but her version didn't include the final page of the hidden cargo. Kirsten flushed with anger and confusion when she saw it.

"Gabriel is a smuggler and an assassin," Mr Fox said as Kirsten looked up from the papers she was reading. His face was neutral. Her composure was calm. She knew about Gabriel's smuggling; she knew about most of the items he brought in. This one shocked her, though.

Mr Fox read her face and then leaned forward. "You know

already."

Kirsten was silent. She dropped her head and nodded. "Not entirely, but some." Kirsten explained that she was aware of the various legal and illegal items that came in with his shipments. She was not aware of Allison or Jeff in Vegas, nor was she aware of the new things he was bringing in. Kirsten put her hand on her head just then and began to rub her temples. It started to throb again.

Mr Fox sat up in his seat when he saw that. "What's wrong?" he asked as he got up and walked around the table to her.

"Just a headache. I'm fine. Why?" Kirsten asked as she adjusted herself and dropped her hand back to the table.

"Is it a regular thing?" Mr Fox asked as he leaned in and looked into her eyes.

"On and off, I guess," Kirsten began. "I don't get them very often, and they go away rather quickly."

"Okay," Mr Fox said as he stood back up and collected the papers in front of her.

"I'm going to head out," Kirsten said as she stood up. "Gabriel will be expecting me soon." Mr Fox just nodded in agreement.

"Take this." Mr Fox handed her a dark hoodie. Kirsten took it and made a questioning face. "For good luck," he finished. Kirsten hugged the hoodie close in her left arm. As she did, she smiled softly at Mr Fox, who winked in response.

"Move carefully," he warned as Kirsten walked to the door. She paused. Almost as if she was going to mentioned something. Nothing was said, however. Mr Fox just stood there in the back of the room.

As Kirsten left, the men with Mr Fox turned to him before one asked, "You didn't show her the info on Allison and Mr

Thompson?"

Mr Fox shook his head in response. "Not yet. I need to be sure before I play all my cards."

"What's next?"

"Keep close tabs on Kirsten and her movements," Mr Fox began. "What she does now will help determine how we need to move going forward." He turned to the first man before continuing, "Get the team ready to move on the warehouse this weekend when the shipment arrives."

Turning to the second, he said, "Watch Kirsten and report back to me directly. And get info on Mr Thompson and the others. Make sure we know where they are the night of the delivery."

When Mr Fox finished, both men got up and left. Mr Fox then gathered the rest of his things before leaving himself. He was formulating a plan about his final moves and how or what he would have to do if Kirsten responded differently. He was even more concerned about what Kirsten would do with the information he had from the texts between Allison and Mr Thompson.

# Chapter 18

# Danger

*Part 1 — Kirsten*

Over the next few days, work went by rather slowly. Kirsten was at a loss now with the new information she received from Mr Fox earlier that week. Secretly, Kirsten had done some digging to see if and when Gabriel or his firm had moved any shipments similar to the one coming in this weekend. She wanted to be sure about what she thought she knew about Gabriel. However, she had come up empty-handed.

Perhaps it was Kirsten's way of trying to convince herself to cut herself off emotionally from Gabriel. Maybe, she was trying to prove to herself that Mr Fox was wrong. No, Mr Fox was rarely wrong. He'd been doing this job for far too long to have given Kirsten info he wasn't sure about. Still, Kirsten struggled with these thoughts as she sat at her desk, thinking about the upcoming weekend.

*Ring! Ring! Ring!*

Kirsten almost jumped as she was snapped out of her thoughts by her desk phone ringing. Kirsten checked the caller's I.D. before answering and saw that it was Mr Thompson. "Hello," she greeted politely.

"Ms Jones," Mr Thompson's chipper voice came through the phone. "How are you doing today?"

"Doing pretty good. How about yourself?"

"Not bad, not bad."

"What can I do for you, Mr Thompson?" Kirsten asked before the conversation got awkward.

Mr Thompson chuckled a bit before answering. "Right to business, I like that." Kirsten rolled her eyes. While trying to avoid an awkward conversation, she had inadvertently created an uncomfortable, and in her mind, unnecessary piece of dialogue and just remained quiet.

Mr Thompson took the cue of Kirsten's silence on the line as he proceeded to explain his business. "Going over the shipments coming in this weekend, I wanted you to be aware that containers 104 — 110 are consolidated with extra freight that isn't on the manifest."

Kirsten acted a bit surprised in her tone. "Oh?" Kirsten, of course, already knew what Mr Thompson was referring to, so her surprise was canned. However, she was curious now to see if he would tell Kirsten himself about what it was. This curiosity was short-lived, though, as Mr Thompson explained further.

"We have specific buyers coming in to receive that freight right off the ship, so make sure those containers are taken down near our warehouse instead of to the trucking depot." Mr Thompson finished speaking, and Kirsten realized that that was all she would get.

"Will do," Kirsten answered as neutrally as possible.

"Much appreciated," Mr Thompson said. "Are you going to be at the docks to help?"

"I'm not sure yet," Kirsten answered. She wasn't sure if she should be there, knowing that Mr Fox had things planned. But then again, maybe she should, so she could keep any suspicions of her away. "If everything is set up right, then I'll probably pass. If it looks like there'll be an issue, then I'll have to be there to ensure a smooth transition," she continued. "Unless Gabriel says otherwise."

"Sounds good. Thank you." And with that, Mr Thompson hung up the phone.

Kirsten leaned back in her chair and exhaled heavily. She wasn't sure how to play this now. After a few minutes, she decided to let Mr Fox handle it instead. Kirsten pulled out her phone and called the most recent number for Mr Fox's phone. He answered right away, which surprised Kirsten somewhat, but she shook that thought to explain what was happening at the docks with the shipments this weekend. Mr Fox took all the information down very carefully and thanked Kirsten for her efforts.

Kirsten hung up and stared down at her desk; she had a shipping manifest from this weekend on it, and she glanced through it again. Nothing but the usual electronics for Gabriel's firm, Pharmaceuticals for Mr Thompson's company, along with some miscellaneous freight. The last page that Kirsten had looked like it should be the last page since it had weight and cost totals for the shipment.

"How do they hide the other things?" Kirsten questioned to herself. All the other times that smuggled items had been brought in, it was carefully split in the numbers column but omitted in the items list. But this one, missing a whole page, and it didn't look like it was hidden in the numbers anywhere on this manifest. Given the type of cargo, this was going to be hard to explain.

After a few minutes, Kirsten couldn't take it anymore and called Gabriel. After ringing several times, she got no answer. *"Strange,"* she thought as she pulled up her computer and checked his schedule. He should just be in his office today. Kirsten called Gabriel's desk phone again, with no answer. Kirsten figured she would have to text him.

*'Hey, babe! I got a question for you when you get a chance.'*
— *Kirsten*

No immediate response. Kirsten decided to freshen up and stretch her legs while she waited. No sooner had she reached the bathroom down the hall when her phone's text notification went off.

*'Sure, what's up?'* — *Gabriel*
*'Are you in your office?'* — *Kirsten*
*'Just got back in, had a quick ZOOM meeting with some of my buyers for this weekend.'* — *Gabriel*
*'Okay, I'll call you.'* — *Kirsten*
*'Cool.'* — *Gabriel*

Kirsten had just finished sending that last message as she reached her desk. She then quickly dialed up to Gabriel's. He answered immediately. "Hello," Gabriel's voice was calm but playful, and Kirsten couldn't help but smile softly.

"Hello," Kirsten greeted in a playful, seductive tone. Gabriel chuckled softly in response. "So," Kirsten got serious again so she could continue. "Mr Thompson called and mentioned that containers 104-110 were to be sent to our warehouse for buyers instead of to the trucking yard for regular distribution."

"And?" Gabriel asked.

"Well, I don't see anything on the manifest about the freight that those containers would have like I normally do."

"Don't worry about it. I've already taken care of that with the ship and the port authorities. This is a one-time shipment and won't be part of our regular hauls. But the money on this one was too good, especially since we already have clear docks," Gabriel explained.

"Gotcha," Kirsten said, not wanting to push the issue much more. "That's all I needed. I'll see you tonight."

"For sure. See you tonight, babe. I love you."

"Love you, too," Kirsten sighed as she hung up. She knew she would have to face the reality of this soon. She just wasn't ready yet.

*Part 2 — Mr Fox*

Mr Fox had been planning for the upcoming weekend in his own way. He had his men watching Kirsten closer and using the bugs Kirsten planted in Mr Thompson's condo to better plan his move against him and Gabriel. Mr Fox would lead the primary team to take the docks, while his counterparts would take Mr Thompson in his office.

Mr Thompson would stay relatively clear of the main action since he was the primary face of one of the legitimate businesses in this collaboration and a coward. Based on what Mr Fox had gathered so far, Mr Thompson was an influential player but stayed as a background player in this operation.

Mr Fox had taken the information about the shipment from Kirsten and added it to his plan. This change would work in his favor, getting the buyers and Gabriel and shipment all at once. Mr Fox sent all his findings up to his superiors for review and permission to proceed. It would be a day or so before he would get a firm answer back from them, which was fine because, in the meantime, he could keep a close watch on Kirsten over the next few days.

Mr Fox was lost in his thoughts for a moment when his phone notification went off. He snapped out of his thoughts and grabbed his phone out of his pocket. It was Kirsten again. *"Strange,"* he thought. Mr Fox had kept their interaction limited since she was more involved with Gabriel and his business. So, since Kirsten had just contacted him about the updates with the shipment coming this weekend, it seemed strange that she would text now unless it were an emergency. Mr Fox opened up the screen to read the text. His eyes showed slight shock but also relief as he read Kirsten's message.

'I'm leaving Gabriel. I'm done. Do what you need to this weekend, I won't be a part of it.' — Kirsten

'Be safe. And remember our quick distress text. If anything goes wrong when you do this. Send me the text, and I'll be there in a hurry.' — Mr Fox

'I will, and yes. I remember what it is. I'll update you after I talk with Gabriel.' — Kirsten

'I will be standing by.' — Mr Fox

As he put his phone away, Mr Fox exhaled heavily and just stood looking out his office window. He was proud of Kirsten. She had been a great help to his operation, and he couldn't have done some of it without her. But he wasn't stupid, he knew how Kirsten felt about Allison and Gabriel, and he knew that as his plan came to a close, Kirsten would be caught in the middle.

He hoped that when the time came, she would make the right call and walk away. A few times Mr Fox thought he might lose Kirsten, but this text showed him there was still some of the real Kirsten inside. As calm as he was about Kirsten's decision, he was also anxious. He was thinking back to the text thread between Allison and Mr Thompson and his knowledge of Gabriel's involvement with Allison's death and Jeff Thomas. He could only hope that she would be safe and Gabriel would just let her walk.

## Part 3 — Kirsten

Kirsten was leaving work when she texted Mr Fox about her plan to break up with Gabriel. Her thoughts kept going back and forth despite the clear evidence about who Gabriel really was and what he'd done. She loved him and was ready to spend her life as part of his life. A portion of her didn't care about whatever Gabriel had done or was doing. Try as she might, Kirsten found it rather challenging to make a decision.

During the drive home, Kirsten decided that she would wait until Saturday to break up with Gabriel. That way, over the next day, she could stay close to make sure any last-minute details would be captured and sent to Mr Fox. *"Should I tell him that I plan on waiting to break up with Gabriel?"* Kirsten thought as she drove. Her text to Mr Fox earlier was rather vague about when she was planning to do it. It could even be taken as she was going to do it tonight.

Kirsten thought through her plan some more and decided that she would just let it ride out; the fewer people that knew of her exact plans, the better. Not that she was concerned about Gabriel finding out from Mr Fox, but she just wanted to be extra safe.

Once she got home, she went up the elevator to her and Gabriel's floor. Kirsten wasn't sure if Gabriel would be home yet. His schedule varied a bit, so sometimes he would be home before Kirsten, other times later in the evening. Today, however, Kirsten hoped it was the latter. She wanted some time to think more, and in a way, brace herself for Gabriel's arrival.

*Ding!* The soft ring of the elevator sounded as she reached her floor. As the doors opened, Kirsten was slightly disheartened as she saw that Gabriel was there already. She smiled softly as he came out of the living room to greet her. Kirsten met him with a gentle hug and a kiss. "How was your day?" he asked as Kirsten put her things away.

"Pretty good," Kirsten responded. She walked into the

bedroom and started to change her clothes. Kirsten thought about just breaking up right there. It was too intense for her. Seeing Gabriel just now, feeling his touch and that smell. Every time Kirsten smelled his cologne, it was like she just gave up on logical thought. She knew she needed to break up with him and leave before the weekend, she knew that it was probably going to be a permanent end, but Kirsten struggled with accepting the action required to make it happen.

Gabriel had followed her into the bedroom. Kirsten had just gotten out of her work clothes as Gabriel came up behind her and hugged her. Kirsten softened as she leaned back into his arms and rested her head on her shoulders. Gabriel started to kiss her neck as they gently swayed back and forth in each other's arms.

Kirsten stopped and turned to face Gabriel. Tears started to form up in her eyes as she looked up into his. Gabriel's body language changed as he became more rigid. "What's wrong?" Gabriel asked. His tone was firm but soft.

After a brief pause, Kirsten finally said, "I'm leaving... I can't do this anymore. We're done." The tears came harder now, and Kirsten quickly grabbed some jeans and a shirt.

Gabriel just stood there for a minute before responding, "Why?"

Kirsten got dressed and then grabbed the hooded sweatshirt that Mr Fox had given her. As she put that on, she managed to suck up the tears a little bit. She didn't answer Gabriel's question. She couldn't even if she wanted to.

She had no way to explain how she knew about the shipment tonight, and any other legitimate reason would reveal too much and probably cause the whole thing to blow up before anyone was ready. Gabriel pleaded again to get an answer from her. But Kirsten just grabbed her purse and keys and headed for the elevator.

Gabriel followed but stopped short as Kirsten entered the elevator and turned to face him as she hit the button. Tears started to form up again, and Kirsten just mouthed a silent goodbye. The door closed, and Gabriel stood for a brief moment before heading to the emergency stairs.

While in the elevator, Kirsten sent a text to Mr Fox.

*'It's done. I left. Good luck tomorrow night.'* — *Kirsten*

Kirsten didn't need to care about a response. She put her phone back in her pocket and tried to keep her composure. Once out of the elevator in the parking area, Kirsten headed straight to her car. As she did, Gabriel came out the stairwell door and called out to her. Kirsten didn't acknowledge him and just kept walking.

"Kirsten!" Gabriel's tone became almost angry. Kirsten glanced over her shoulder to see that Gabriel was walking quickly behind her. She pulled out her phone and quickened her pace.

Gabriel was still calling out as he quickened his pace to match Kirsten's. As Kirsten got to her car, she saw Gabriel in the window reflection behind her. Suddenly, his arms wrapped around her. She immediately struggled and began to fight back. In the struggle, she dropped her phone as she attempted to use it to call for help.

Before she could get a good hit in, a cloth was held over her face. Her body softened as she realized she was going to sleep. "You're not allowed to leave," Gabriel's voice was clear and firm. It was the last thing she heard as she slumped in unconsciousness.

# Chapter 19

## Identity

Mr Fox put his phone down after reading Kirsten's text. A huge feeling of relief swept over him momentarily. He knew that this would put Kirsten at risk now until this operation was over. Hopefully, she would remain safe until then.

Mr Fox then called his men to tell them of the new development. "Put your teams together for the raid tomorrow night," he said on the phone with them. "I'll take the warehouse and Gabriel. You two take Mr Thompson and the others."

"Are all the warrants ready?" asked one of the men.

"Yes, they'll be sent to you directly beforehand," Mr Fox replied.

"Good. We'll get prepped and be on standby for the 'go ahead'," the man said.

After a brief goodbye, Mr Fox got his things together to be ready for tomorrow night. He hoped Kirsten would reach out again to let him know where she would be and that she was safe. But it looked like he would have just to trust her on this one. Kirsten could take care of herself well enough. Mr Fox knew this.

However, the emotional trauma that was sure to develop, if it hadn't already, was what he was more concerned about. That said, perhaps that's why she didn't reach out. In an attempt to keep herself distant from the events going on to help her cope and heal. Whatever the reason, Mr Fox trusted Kirsten to do the right thing, and she had so far. Now, it was up to him and his team to finish this and end it once and for all.

...A cold chill was felt, and the room felt slightly damp. As her vision returned, Kirsten realized that she couldn't move her arms or legs and felt pain around her face. Glancing around, she noticed she was tied up, gagged and propped against a wall. She noticed that she was in the warehouse at the docks.

A cluster of voices was heard. Kirsten looked over in their direction. She couldn't make out what was said, but she did recognize them as Gabriel and the others he worked with. They talked on the other side of the warehouse near the loading dock door when she fully came to. Their backs were turned against her direction, so Kirsten tried to wrestle free very carefully. However, no matter what she tried, she couldn't get into a position to begin to cut or remove the bonds.

After a few moments of struggling, Kirsten noticed her stomach was growling loudly. The realization came that made her realize that she hadn't eaten since who knows when. That thought, of course, led to her wondering how long she had been out. The last thing she remembers was her leaving Gabriel's when he jumped her.

Suddenly, Kirsten noticed the men on the other side of the warehouse had turned to look in her direction. Kirsten's stirring was enough to attract the attention of the men who were in the warehouse with her. One of the men walked over. As he got closer, Kirsten noticed that he was one of the board members in Mr Thompson's company.

The man approached and stood over Kirsten. He was tall, but here, seemed much taller while Kirsten was tied and lying on the floor. The man just stood still for a moment as Kirsten's thoughts raced about what was going on and what he was going to do.

Then, without warning, the man reached behind Kirsten and very roughly rolled her over on her stomach. Kirsten tried to cry out, but all that was heard were muffled screams with the gag in her mouth.

Kirsten was pinned on her stomach. Her face was pressed into the cold, dirty floor. She felt the man groping her, but with her arms and hands tied up back there, combined with the numbing sensation she had from being held in the same position for so long, she couldn't tell what exactly the man was doing.

Kirsten felt her hands go free. She relaxed a little as she felt the blood and feeling return to her fingers. The man then released the ropes on her ankles, and then using the ropes that still bound her arms behind her, the man pulled Kirsten up to her feet. His grip was rough and firm. Kirsten thought about trying to run or fight but realized before she even finished that thought that she was far too weak to attempt such a thing yet.

"Are you going to make it?" the man asked almost sarcastically. Both fear and determination could be seen in Kirsten's eyes. The man just smiled as he forced Kirsten to walk to a nearby table and sit down in a chair there. The other men joined at this time and helped tie Kirsten's ankles to each leg of the chair; her torso was also tied after. Then the rope that held her arms to her sides was released and the gag removed.

Two of the men stood on either side of Kirsten as she sat there. The other, the one who moved Kirsten from the floor to this chair, sat across from her and placed a plate of food in front of her. Kirsten looked at it but wasn't sure of the implication, and so, she did nothing.

"Eat," the man said, gesturing to the plate in front of her. Kirsten didn't move. Smiling, the man then grabbed one of the apple slices and bit into it himself. "See?" he asked, eating the fruit. "It's not poison. If Gabriel wanted you dead, he would've done it when he grabbed you," he continued. "You need your strength. Eat." His tone was firmer this time as if he had been ordered to make sure Kirsten was fed.

Not seeing a way out at the moment and feeling so hungry, Kirsten slowly and cautiously started to eat. The food felt so good. Kirsten couldn't remember if she had ever been this hungry before. She tried to pace herself, so she didn't give the impression that she was that hungry. After she cleaned the plate, Kirsten drank the whole bottle of water sitting there.

After a few moments, despite being tied up yet, Kirsten began to feel better. There was an awkward silence for several minutes before the man spoke again.

"Who are you working for?" he asked directly. Kirsten remained calm but gave a curious expression.

The man leaned forward in his seat. The two behind Kirsten took a step forward. "Who are you working for?" he asked again in the same tone.

"Gabriel?" Kirsten asked.

The man leaned back in his seat. "We know that you are infiltrating our operation. We know that you have ties to law enforcement." He paused before going any further. Kirsten just sat there silently; she didn't know how much they knew already, and she wasn't about to give them anything more.

"Our regular informant went missing some time ago," the man said. His tone was calmer and more casual now. He adjusted himself in his seat to get more comfortable. His gaze never left Kirsten's as he waited to see how she would react. He would be disappointed, however, as Kirsten remained steady and silent. She was merely glaring back at him with a calm yet defiant look.

This interrogation went on for some time before the man

finally stopped when his phone vibrated. He reached into the breast pocket of his jacket to get it out. The man's face changed when he realized who was calling, and he quickly cleared his throat and stood up to answer it.

"Yes, sir?" he greeted quickly. There was a long pause while he listened to whoever was on the other end of the line. Kirsten glanced up at the men on either side of her. They didn't move or even acknowledge her. The man on the phone was pacing casually across the table, occasionally nodding as he listened.

"She hasn't said anything yet," the man said into the phone. He stopped and glanced in at Kirsten. "Yes, she ate and drank the water provided," he continued. He nodded at the two men by Kirsten and then turned and walked further away to continue his conversation.

The two men grabbed Kirsten, roughly untied her from the chair, and re-tied her ankles and hands. Once she was bound and gagged again, the men carried her into one of the storage closets against the wall near where Kirsten was tied up before.

The men dropped her in the center of the small room. Kirsten let out a soft grunt as she hit the floor. "Try to relax," the one man said. "You'll be here a while yet." Kirsten just rolled to her side and faced the men in the doorway. Nothing more was said, and after a moment, the men left the room, closing the door behind them. Kirsten heard what sounded like a bolt or bar being set outside, effectively locking her in...

...*Meanwhile.*

Mr Fox had been finalizing his plans with his men, going over the last of the details. He had already discretely confirmed with the shipping yard the particulars of Gabriel's shipment coming in tonight, and thanks to the bugs planted in Mr

Thompson's condo by Kirsten, he had the whereabouts of some of the other members of the board, including Mr Thompson. Everything was coming into place. Mr Fox was slightly worried about Kirsten. He hadn't heard anything from her since she sent the message about leaving Gabriel. He had sent a follow check-in text earlier this morning, but no response as of yet.

He could only hope that Kirsten was purposely staying low and would reach out once this was over. If Mr Fox was honest with himself, he felt really bad for Kirsten's situation. He never thought that by putting her in the middle of this, she would end up in a serious relationship with someone who became a significant player in the operation. Nor did he expect the torn friendship with Allison to have been such a problem. Ultimately, however, Mr Fox knew that Kirsten understood the risks, and despite how it turned out, she played her part flawlessly.

Mr Fox had his team stationed out and ready when the ship docked. Snipers in the distance would feed reports through the comm-link that each team member had. The two other team leads Mr Fox had sent to be ready to move in on Mr Thompson and the others at their respective locations.

"We've got movement at the warehouse," a voice came through the earpiece Mr Fox was wearing. Mr Fox put his hand up to his ear as he raised his binoculars to his eyes. He was posted some distance away in the yard to stay close enough to move in quickly but far enough back that they wouldn't be noticed.

As he looked through the lens, Mr Fox noticed that the shipping containers had reached the warehouse as they were backed into the unloading dock of the building. Mr Fox saw a few men outside directing the trucks. Each one backed into the appropriate docking door against the warehouse. Once in place, Mr Fox continued to observe as the men disconnected from the trailers and drove the cabs back down the docks towards the shipyard.

"Hold position, men," Mr Fox's voice came through the earpieces of the team very clearly. "We want the buyers too. They should be showing up soon."

Mr Fox looked around the dock as best he could in the fading light of the sunset. He couldn't see Gabriel or any of the others that were supposed to be there tonight. "Stiles," he called one of the snipers by his last name.

"Sir," came the acknowledgment through the earpiece.

"Switch to infrared. Give me a body count." Mr Fox had dropped the binoculars away from his eyes to better take in the whole picture. This was his chance to finish this, and he wasn't going to let it fail.

"Yes, sir," Stiles answered. "Switching to infrared."

"What do you see?" Mr Fox asked after a few moments.

"Four bodies in the warehouse. They seem to be standing near the loading dock doors," Stiles began. "Wait a minute... Sir, we have five bodies in the warehouse."

"Confirm five," Mr Fox said.

"Five confirmed," Stiles answered. "The fifth body is in a separate room. It almost looks like they're lying down."

Mr Fox's face tightened as he heard the report. "Scan the trucks."

"I got a dozen bodies, or so I'm reading in each one," Stiles replied after a few minutes.

*"Good,"* Mr Fox thought. *"At least we have that."* Speaking into his mic now, Mr Fox asked Stiles to focus on the warehouse again. He was curious about that fifth body seen away from the others.

Unfortunately, Stiles didn't have any new information about

the individual. "He's still in the same spot," he stated. "Hard to see in this view, but it almost looks like the individual is tied up."

Mr Fox's thoughts froze. Immediately he ran through the list of personnel he had in both his team and the people he was watching. He was trying to figure out who might have gone unnoticed that Gabriel would even have restrained. The mole had been taken care of some time ago. He quickly asked his team leads to do an accountability check. All came back clear and good to go. Mr Fox thought for a moment while they waited for the buyers to show up. He considered calling Kirsten but changed his mind as he continued to look out the window where he was. If it was her, he'd be putting her and his team in greater risk by trying to make contact.

"Stiles," Mr Fox finally said.

"Yes, sir?" came the quick response.

You wouldn't know it just by listening through the mic, but Mr Fox was deeply concerned by this development. "Keep watching that warehouse and let me know if anything changes with that individual on the floor," he said as calmly as possible. He then relayed to the team leads about a possible hostage situation.

Now, it was truly a waiting game...

*"Where are they?"* Mr Fox muttered to himself. The sun was just below the horizon, and the dock lights had turned on to illuminate the area. No activity or sudden change with Gabriel or his men. The buyers hadn't shown up yet, and while he had enough to take out Gabriel and his whole operation on its own, the idea that he could get a few more big players by catching the buyers as well was too good to pass up.

"Sir! We've got movement in the warehouse." Stile's voice in the earpiece knocked Mr Fox out of his thoughts as he trained the binoculars back out on the dock. "One of the men has grabbed the figure that was on the floor and is dragging them out near the others," Stiles finished saying.

"All teams hold fast," Mr Fox said in his mic quickly as he noticed several vehicles show up. "Stiles, continue to monitor the situation. Everyone else get into position. The buyers are here."

"Yes, sir!"

*...Meanwhile.*

Kirsten wasn't sure how long she'd been lying there. Her wrists and ankles were chafed raw, and she had to stop struggling against the binds from the pain and discomfort. Her head was pounding, she wasn't sure if it was stress or what, but the headache didn't help her situation. Distorted voices could be heard. She couldn't make out any familiar voices, nor could Kirsten discern what they were saying. The warehouse was old, but it was kept rather well, so all the walls and ceiling were in good condition.

Suddenly the door opened, and Kirsten recognized the man as the one that put her in the room before. Before she could even react, the man had grabbed her and began to drag her out into the central area of the warehouse.

Kirsten squinted at the light as she was carried, albeit only partially. She was still mostly dragged across the floor. As her vision cleared, she saw the men more clearly. She didn't see Mr Thompson; however, she recognized all the men there as members of Gabriel's company. Kirsten was forcefully seated in a chair in the center of the floor. It was an awkward position since her hands and feet were still bound. The man that put her there remained behind her, watching closely. No one else acknowledged her or even looked at her.

Before long, some of the other men started to open the dock doors revealing the cargo trailers parked in the stalls. Then, from the back of the warehouse came a familiar figure. Kirsten trained her neck to get a better look at who was walking towards the group. It was Gabriel. As he approached the chair where Kirsten was sitting, he smiled. His usual soft smile greeted Kirsten as though nothing had happened. Then, as he got next to her, the soft, friendly smile changed to a cold, coy smile.

He stopped just short of Kirsten, crouching down till he was more at eye level with her. His cologne was strong, and Kirsten immediately felt a sense of calmness. Thankfully, having her hands and legs bound with a gag tied around her mouth helped conceal her reaction.

Gabriel didn't say anything at first, just looked at her. Then, he gently brushed some of her hair away from Kirsten's face. His smile softened again as he stood and said, "I had hoped that we could've avoided this moment."

"What's the plan?" the man standing behind Kirsten asked plainly.

"She'll be bundled in with the rest," Gabriel answered as he walked to the loading docks checking his watch. "They should be arriving shortly."

It would only be a few minutes when the warehouse's front door opened, and several men and women in expensive-looking suits walked in. Gabriel greeted them, and they chatted briefly as he directed them to the area they would be standing in. Nodding to the men closest to the doors, they began unlocking the trailers but leaving them closed.

"Welcome. Ladies and gentlemen," Gabriel started to say. "Tonight, we are starting what will hopefully be a long and prosperous collaboration."

Gabriel finished speaking just as the front door burst in. The swat team had entered and made a quick line to secure points of entry. In the commotion, Gabriel remained calm and quickly grabbed Kirsten, picked her up and forced her to stand in front of him. All the buyers scattered in a panic. But at every turn, more agents were surrounding them, closing in guns ready.

"Mr Ramirez," Mr Fox spoke clearly as he stepped through the agents, gun drawn. "DHS." He stopped just a few feet away from Gabriel, who was still holding Kirsten in front as a human shield. "You are all under arrest," he finished. Gabriel's men had their guns out. Even some of the buyers had their weapons drawn. They were outnumbered, but everyone was paused in a standoff.

Gabriel didn't move. His facial expression didn't change. Mr Fox remained calm and steady. Kirsten was glancing back and forth, Gabriel had a gun hidden against her back, and Mr Fox had the gun pointed at Gabriel but with her body in the way. She tried to think, but her brain was going a million miles an hour. Then suddenly, the silence broke. "What are you going to do?" Gabriel finally asked. "Let me go, or I'll kill her. I know that you've somehow recruited her against me."

"You're both correct and wrong," Mr Fox said smoothly. He never missed a beat. Turning to Kirsten now, he asked, "Are you all right, Ms Campbell?" Kirsten nodded in a quick short head jerk.

"Campbell?" Gabriel exclaimed. He glanced down at Kirsten and back up at Mr Fox. He tightened his grip on Kirsten and pushed the gun deeper into her back.

"Yes," Mr Fox interjected. "Agent Kimberly Campbell. I never recruited her against you. She was always working for me," he continued. "And your operation is closed. Permanently." Mr Fox took a step closer as he finished.

Gabriel's face tensed even more. In a rage, he shoved Kimberly in Mr Fox's direction. Mr Fox didn't even flinch. With her ankles still tied, Kimberly tripped right away and began to fall forward.

*Bang! Bang!*

Two shots rang out. Kimberly felt a pain in her back as she hit the ground. Falling somewhat on her side, she laid there, not moving.

*Bang! Bang!*

Two more shots rang out as fast as the first two. After a pause, Gabriel dropped his gun. He glanced down as blood trickled through his shirt. Mr Fox's gun was still smoking as he lowered it. Gabriel collapsed on the spot. "But she didn't want to go against you," Mr Fox muttered.

Seeing their leader fall, the rest of the men voluntarily dropped their weapons, and the agents quickly moved in to subdue the prisoners. The buyers were rounded up as well, and all were handcuffed and led into the swat truck outside.

As his men handled the others, Mr Fox crouched down and began to untie Kimberly. Once her hands and legs were free, he tapped her face to wake her up. Once Kimberly's eye's opened, Mr Fox smiled and called for a medic. "Good thing you wore that sweater," he said, chuckling as he did. Pulling his hand out from underneath her, he held one of the bullets that had shot Kimberly from Gabriel's gun. "Lodged in the Kevlar lining."

Kimberly just smiled and gave a small chuckle. At this time, the medics arrived and began to check her over. Mr Fox stood up, and one of his men came up to him. "We just got word that Mr Thompson and the others have been apprehended as well."

"Good," Mr Fox responded. He walked over to the dock doors where the trailers were still sitting. Turning to a couple of the men closest to him, he gestured and said, "Let's open 'em up."

# Chapter 20

## Secrets Out

The men began to open the trailer doors. Mr Fox just stood there gazing at the boxes that were stacked up immediately inside the containers. The men were directed to unload the boxes right away. Each one was stamped with *Thompson Pharmaceuticals*. Nothing out of the ordinary was found within those particular boxes. However, Mr Fox wasn't concerned with those at the moment.

Once most of the boxes had been removed from one of the trailers, Mr Fox was already inside trying to find the false compartment. As each box was taken out, you could tell that the interior wasn't the same size as the exterior. Mr Fox had a few men come in to help as they searched for any hidden latches. "Here!" one of the men finally said. As Mr Fox rushed over, the man was already pulling a small pin out of a crevice in the wall rivet.

As he did so, the interior wall shifted, just enough that Mr Fox was able to grab it and pull it open. As he did, he and the other men shined their flashlights in to reveal the secret cargo that Gabriel had brought in. "There's got to be a couple dozen at least," one of the men said. Mr Fox just nodded in agreement.

Inside was several women. Ages ranged from what appeared to be early teens to mid-thirties. All of them looked very dirty. "How long do you think they've been locked in here?" one of the men asked.

"The whole trip," Mr Fox said solemnly. "Let's get them out," he said he stepped out of that trailer and stepped into the next one. It was the same, every container. They all had a dozen or so women of primarily Asian descent taken from who knows where.

When confronted with the lights, the women crouched down. Mr Fox and his men began to try and communicate with them to help them understand that they were there to help. Most of the women only understood a few words in English. It was enough to get them to come out and not be totally afraid, but Mr Fox knew he would need some help and called for a translator and immigration to help with the process.

Red and blue flashing lights reflected off the buildings and containers, along with the bright headlights as well as the overhead dock lights that lit up the area. Mr Fox just stood silent for a few minutes as he surveyed the scene. Various police officers were bustling about. The occasional camera flash would drown out the other lights as the crime scene team gathered photographic evidence. A few E.M.T.s were gathering their equipment to assist those already inside and treating the victims that came off the trailers.

Mr Fox made his way to one of the ambulances; Agent Kimberly was seated there with her shirt and sweater pulled up to her shoulders to reveal her back. The medic was examining the contact points of the bullet shots that hit her. Mr Fox made eye contact with her as he approached though Kimberly could only acknowledge him with her eyes since her nose and mouth were covered by the oxygen mask she was holding up to her face.

"How is she?" Mr Fox asked the medic. Kimberly pulled the mask away and shot him an annoyed look. Mr Fox just smiled in response but kept his attention on the medic that was attending to her.

"She'll be fine," the medic said. "Thankfully, the bullets hit her at an angle, so the Kevlar lining was able to keep them from penetrating. However, the impact still caused some surface bruising, a little internal bruising around the left kidney and a fractured rib," he finished speaking as he connected the wrap around Kimberly's rib just below her chest.

Kimberley sat up carefully and pulled her shirt and sweater down. Kimberly stood up as the medic began to clean up. Kimberly made a painful grimace as she tried to take a step forward. The medic quickly jumped in, but Mr Fox was first and waved him back. "Are you going to make it?" he asked her.

Kimberly nodded. "The adrenaline is just wearing off." Mr Fox continued to help her into the back of the S.U.V.

"Take a few days. We'll touch base later, to set up your debrief," he said as Kimberly got comfortable in the seat. Mr Fox glanced behind him. "We'll have enough to do in the meantime to finish this out." Kimberly nodded, and with that, Mr Fox shut the door and waved off the driver. He stood and watched as the S.U.V. pulled away, the bustle of the scene still rushing around him.

Mr Fox was lost in thought for a moment when a voice broke through. "Sir," one of the officers yelled as he walked up to Mr Fox. He turned to greet the approaching uniforms. "Sir," the officer repeated. "We found it." Mr Fox promptly followed him back into the warehouse.

When they got inside, the officer took Mr Fox over to the trailers. Several men were around them, some counting boxes, others photographing everything, and some were still unloading and sorting what was found. Amongst all the freight that was pulled out was a small collection of unmarked boxes. Another officer was crouched down, examining some of the items in one of the boxes. As Mr Fox came up to him, the man stood up and handed him one of the packets as he greeted, "Sir."

"What do we have?" Mr Fox asked as he took the package

from the officer. The boxes on the floor themselves were unmarked. However, the smaller boxes inside were stamped with *Thompson Pharmaceuticals,* and inside each one, were several containers of a currently unknown clear liquid substance. "Any indication on what this is?" Mr Fox said to the man as he handed back the containers he had.

"Not yet," the man said as he placed the container back in the box. "But it is part of the unlisted freight, and if it matches with what we found over a year ago, this will connect everyone." He finished speaking, and Mr Fox nodded in agreement.

Turning to the other officer, he said, "Make sure the lab gets this and puts a rush on it."

"Yes, sir."

Mr Fox then turned to check on the others and verify the evidence list. He was grateful this was over and had this part of the smuggling issue taken care of. He sat down on some pallets outside the warehouse as the crew started to thin out. The arrested individuals were already driven out to be processed. The captive women were gone and being taken care of by immigration. The coroner was gone along with most of the swat team. Kimberly should be resting at home by now, and while the last of the freight was being tagged and loaded, it gave him time to reflect on everything that led up to this.

As he compiled his thoughts, Mr Fox knew that Kimberly would need to be debriefed and filled in on everything. Additionally, he was concerned about how her transition back to reality would be. It wasn't an easy process, and for some, it was more challenging than others — one piece at a time.

# Chapter 21

## Questions Answered

The room was cold; at least, it felt cold to her. Perhaps she wasn't as recovered as she thought from the gunshot wounds in her back. Maybe, she was coming down with something. Flu season was approaching. It could be that. Her elbows rested on the table in front of her, and her head rested in her hands. The room was just a briefing room, standard conference table and chairs all around — simple yet pleasant office décor on the walls.

The door to the room suddenly opened. "Ms Campbell?" said a familiar voice. The voice, of course, belonged to Mr Fox, and although the sudden entrance startled her, she didn't move or flinch at his entrance.

"Kimberly," Mr Fox said again as he sat down across the table from her. His tone was softer but still firm.

*"Kimberly,"* she thought. It was her name, but it didn't feel like her name. She hadn't heard it in a long time. A flash of her life came to her as she sat there. Gabriel, Allison, her apartment, the gym, her old life; no one ever talks about the struggle to return to reality in these situations. Almost two years of her life were spent as Kirsten Jones, but now, it was over. She played a role, yet despite her best efforts, she couldn't just shake it off. She was unable to tell which life was real and which was fake correctly.

Mr Fox was glancing through the papers in the file he brought in and set in front of him. Kimberly glanced up and drew a deep breath. Relaxing a bit now and settling in her chair, she faced Mr Fox and waited. Mr Fox merely glanced up for a moment at Kimberly before looking back at the file. "If you're not ready to be back, you can take more time," he said softly.

She thought for a moment. But what would that accomplish? More time away meant a more extended time until she'd have the answers that she needed to close this chapter. It's not like time at home was helping her nerves with all this. She was still processing the return to the life of Kimberly Campbell. No, she needed to be here to ease back into work and get the closure she needed from this case. Kimberly just shook her head. "I may take some time later, but I need to make sure this is wrapped up and finished before I can relax."

"Fair enough," Mr Fox said, exhaling heavily before continuing. "Eighteen months," he said finally picking his eyes up off the pages in front of him. Kimberly didn't move; she was anxiously waiting for this to be over so she could finally relax and let it go. "That's a long time for someone to be undercover," Mr Fox continued. "But I must say you did an excellent job," he finished.

"So, what's the full story here?" Kimberly asked plainly. She was eager to see what pieces Mr Fox had put together from the outside while she was still inside playing the game.

Mr Fox explained that Mr Thompson was the intended target from the beginning. He used his pharmaceutical company shipments to hide black market items in his containers. Initially, they'd deemed this a relatively easy and cut case. However, as they'd learned later, he wasn't alone, and Mr Fox and the DHS wanted all the snakeheads at once.

Allison was then found by the agent, who would later be found to be a mole for Mr Thompson and Gabriel. Kimberly was to go undercover and get close to Allison so Mr Fox could get info on the others involved. At this point for security, Mr Fox and Kimberly had never met. Each was a part of different units within the DHS, and it was best that, at least at first, they didn't have any known correspondence.

Kimberly shifted in her seat as Mr Fox continued. Kirsten Jones was then created and set in place. They knew it would take some time before contact with Allison would be made, so, in the meantime, Mr Fox and his team had broadened out their information gathering on Mr Thompson's associates.

Mr Fox continued to speak as Kimberly drowned him out with her own thoughts. She already knew all this; her job was to go undercover and be a target for Allison and hope that she would give out some pieces of the puzzle and allow her and Mr Fox to connect the dots through their friendship. One thing that wasn't counted on was Gabriel. Kimberly still didn't know why Allison set her up with him, nor why she herself had fallen for him so quickly and thoroughly. Kimberly expected that her friendship with Allison would lead to just a casual friendship and shared information. But as fast as that spiral went out of control after Gabriel showed up, Kimberly had a hard time believing that there wasn't more to that side of the story.

Especially after what she did with him and how Allison broke the relationship, there seemed initially no rhyme or reason why Allison would go through all the trouble of getting Gabriel and her together if she was only going to break it up herself later. With Allison's position in the company and her connection to the smuggling, it seemed strange that she would invite Kirsten in, especially since they assumed the mole was feeding information to them from near the beginning.

Whether she suspected Kimberly's cover as Kirsten to be a

ruse or not was irrelevant. The fact remained that it jeopardized the whole operation by having Kimberly get that close to Allison's group. Unfortunately, her death effectively eliminated any chance she had of retrieving that explanation from Allison. Hopefully, something in today's info from Mr Fox would perhaps fill in some of the holes.

"When Gabriel came into the picture, as I mentioned before, he passed our initial background check, and the only tie we could make to Mr Thompson was through Allison and using Gabriel's connections at the docks," Mr Fox explained. Kimberly zoned out for few minutes again when Mr Fox mentioned Allison. This time her thoughts went to the hurt that Allison caused. Kimberly boiled inside. Gabriel was a bad guy and dead now, but she still struggled with her feelings and remembering the pain she felt then made Allison unforgivable. Kimberly was happy she was dead and gone.

"When Gabriel went to Vegas—" Mr Fox's voice broke through Kimberly's thoughts, and she snapped back. *"Vegas,"* she thought, more memories flooded in. Some of Gabriel and then Allison again. Kimberly's muscles tightened. Mr Fox paused a moment. He realized that Kimberly wasn't listening and also saw her grip tighten and face grow tense. "Is everything all right?" he asked.

Kimberly just nodded slowly. "Good," Mr Fox said. Significantly more chipper than he was before, he handed Kimberly a paper out of the file he had. "Then you'll want to read this." Kimberly leaned forward cautiously. After all the twists and turns this case had taken her, she wasn't in the mood to be whiplashed again.

As she started reading the paper, she softened. It would indeed prove to be another twist. What Mr Fox had just handed her was the transcript of the text conversation between Allison and Mr Thompson right before Gabriel left for Vegas. It was also vital to understand how much Gabriel was involved and gave some deeper insight into the relationship between Kirsten and Allison.

'We need to talk.' — Allison

'What's up?' — Mr Thompson

'I don't like this plan to use Kirsten like this.' — Allison

'It doesn't matter what you want.' — Mr Thompson

'It should. I'm on the board and oversee all the manifests. Why can't we test this elsewhere?' — Allison

'Your position is granted to you by my peers. But if you push your limits, I'll have you removed.' — Mr Thompson

'Gabriel won't approve of that. And you know it.' — Allison

'Don't be so sure.' — Mr Thompson

'I'll talk to Gabriel when he comes back from Vegas. But if it doesn't go my way, I'll tell Kirsten everything.' — Allison

'That would be a mistake. And Gabriel is set on Kirsten. You won't convince him easily.' — Mr Thompson

'He's a man, and I'm a woman. He'll do whatever I want if I push the right buttons. I know he's not really in love with Kirsten.' — Allison

'You best be careful.' — Mr Thompson

'Testing your drug on Kirsten through Gabriel is wrong. Even I can't tell if she is actually in love with him or not any more.' — Allison

'That's the point.' — Mr Thompson

'But it might be killing her.' — Allison

'What do you care? Your mole said she's the right one.' — Mr Thompson

'I am not a fan of Gabriel's so-called "big picture plan." So, *what my mole offered is irrelevant, and Kirsten isn't worth this.'* — *Allison*

*'You're all talk, Allison. You don't actually want to ruin anything here. You like your life as it is.'* — *Mr Thompson*

*'Watch me. I will get Gabriel to back off Kirsten and get Kirsten to want to leave at the same time.'* — *Allison*

*'We'll talk when Gabriel gets back.'* — *Mr Thompson*

There wasn't any more to the script. Kimberly just sat there dumbfounded. Allison, was trying to help me? How could... Thoughts of the events of the past year rolled through her brain as if it was yesterday. The pain and love and friendship all rolled in at once. "So, Allison was actually trying to save me by interfering with my relationship?" Kimberly finally said as she put the paper down and looked over at Mr Fox. He was sitting still and unmoved up till now.

"Apparently so," Mr Fox said smoothly. "However, with Gabriel and Allison dead, it's doubtful that we will get the full story on that end. Mr Thompson is only saying so much, and his lawyer has us running in circles right now."

Kimberly sat back and just kept silent. Gabriel wanted her and then used her for Mr Thompson's drug experiment. Then Allison, who had been in with Gabriel the whole time, decided to grow a conscience and break up Kirsten and Gabriel. In doing so, it revealed that Gabriel had real true feelings for Kirsten and caused him to kill Allison to protect it. However, Kimberly never did get beyond that though. *Did Gabriel genuinely love and want her? Or was he just using her for a different purpose yet unrevealed?*

"Your tox screen came back positive for the drug we found in the containers, and it matched with what we found in Gabriel's condo." Mr Fox's voice broke Kimberly's thoughts as he continued. "They used the cologne that Gabriel wore as a means to test the drug, being inhaled little by little every time you were with him. Gabriel had traces of an antibody in his system, which is why it seemed only to affect you. Those headaches you had been experiencing were a side effect of the drug in the system."

Kimberly didn't say anything. She was still hung up on how much was true or not. From her side of the story, it would've seemed that Gabriel just wanted Kirsten, knowing that she was DHS. Perhaps he hoped to have a double agent with Kirsten. Allison, the friend who backstabbed her but then apparently decided that what they wanted with Kirsten was too much and then used those things to break up Gabriel and Kirsten. Though, thinking back now, there was no better way to make that break-up final. Had it been any other relationship, Kirsten would've walked away and ghosted everyone involved.

But here, she didn't. Kimberly still couldn't quite tell why. Did she really love Gabriel? Was it just the drugs? She couldn't tell, and that made her head hurt and her stomach sick. No, the feelings were definitely real. The drug was just the added point to engrain those feelings deeper. You can't make someone love you if they don't want it, but you can enhance the emotions that are already there. Maybe? Kimberly groaned out loud, so many questions, so many feelings.

Mr Fox didn't miss a beat queuing back to his story. "Gabriel's entire network with Mr Thompson has been broken. His connection with the west coast company that was still in progress after Jeff's death in Vegas has been halted. The buyers had lawyered up, but chances are they'd get nailed on something even if it's only minor." He paused momentarily and exhaled heavily. He knew that the answers they wanted he didn't have yet. "Kimberly, I'm afraid based on what we have so far and with

Allison and Gabriel dead, we won't ever truly know why Gabriel picked you and to what end your presence would've been for. Nor will we ever fully understand Allison's actions of bringing you in to only secretly try and get you out by sabotaging your relationship that way."

Kimberly walked down the hallway of the building. Office doors lined the hall, some were open, and some were closed. Kimberly didn't notice much; however, she was still thinking about the whole scenario. *"Take a few weeks off. Your office will be ready for you when you come back."* Mr Fox's last words echoed in her brain. Kimberly didn't know if she'd be ready in a few weeks. She wasn't sure if she'd ever be ready. Her headaches would get less and based on what they knew, there wouldn't be any lasting side effects. She would, of course, be monitored for several months, until they were sure.

*Kimberly Campbell*, the nameplate on the door was clear enough. She entered and sat down behind her desk. Various awards and other certificates were on the walls, some books in a small book self in the corner. Her desk was bare, save for the phone and a computer. Kimberly caught herself still thinking as she sat there. The court process would take a while. They always do. But it looked like they had enough evidence that there wasn't any real need to make any plea deals with anyone, so they should all get the time they deserved. Kimberly's alias was deleted. No trace of Kirsten Jones remained anywhere other than the memories of those who knew her.

Memories, which hung in Kimberly's head like a pungent odor. Heavy and thick. What is it to love and to see through the bad? If she hadn't tried to leave, would Gabriel have attacked her? Would he ever have tried? Kim remembered the conversation she overhead with Gabriel and Allison both times, and both times Gabriel seemed his most sincere about Kirsten. Was there love in there that he felt for her? Did she love him beyond the drug-induced scents? She was a cop, and he was a criminal... Could there ever be true love with that? Or is it true what they say — that Love is Blind?

# End